Capitally Engaged

RACHEL HOLM

ISBN: 9798986576244
ISBN: 9798986576251
https://www.rachelwholm.com/
Cover Design: Books-Design.com
Editor: Lacey Braziel Edits
Proofreader: Weaver Way Author Services

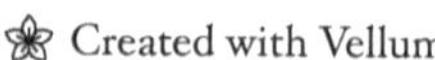 Created with Vellum

A Note from the Author

WHILE THIS IS NOT a book about politics, it does take place against the background of a liberal political workplace. Some political issues and ideologies are referenced.

I did my best to represent accuracy about Senate offices and campaigns, but at times took liberties for "the plot." Any changes are my own and not the reflection of those kind enough to read and give me notes.

Many places referenced in Washington, DC are real, but specific details may be embellished or fictionalized. Anything spoken of negatively is fictional.

This book contains adult language and explicit intimate scenes.

CONTENT NOTES:

Parental death, off page, past (long-term unspecified illness, car accident); Grandparent death off page, past (short-term illness); discussions of grief and impact of loss; unhealthy relationship, past, discussed; gastrointestinal distress, on-page, not overly detailed

Depictions of Irritable Bowel Syndrome are based on my own experiences, but have been read by others who also have lived experience. I did my best to portray the impact of parental loss and grief on forming relationships, and am grateful to those who read with their own experiences in mind to provide feedback. I know not all those who share lived experiences with Jax and Preston will see themselves in these pages, but I hope I have portrayed these topics with the care and respect they deserve.

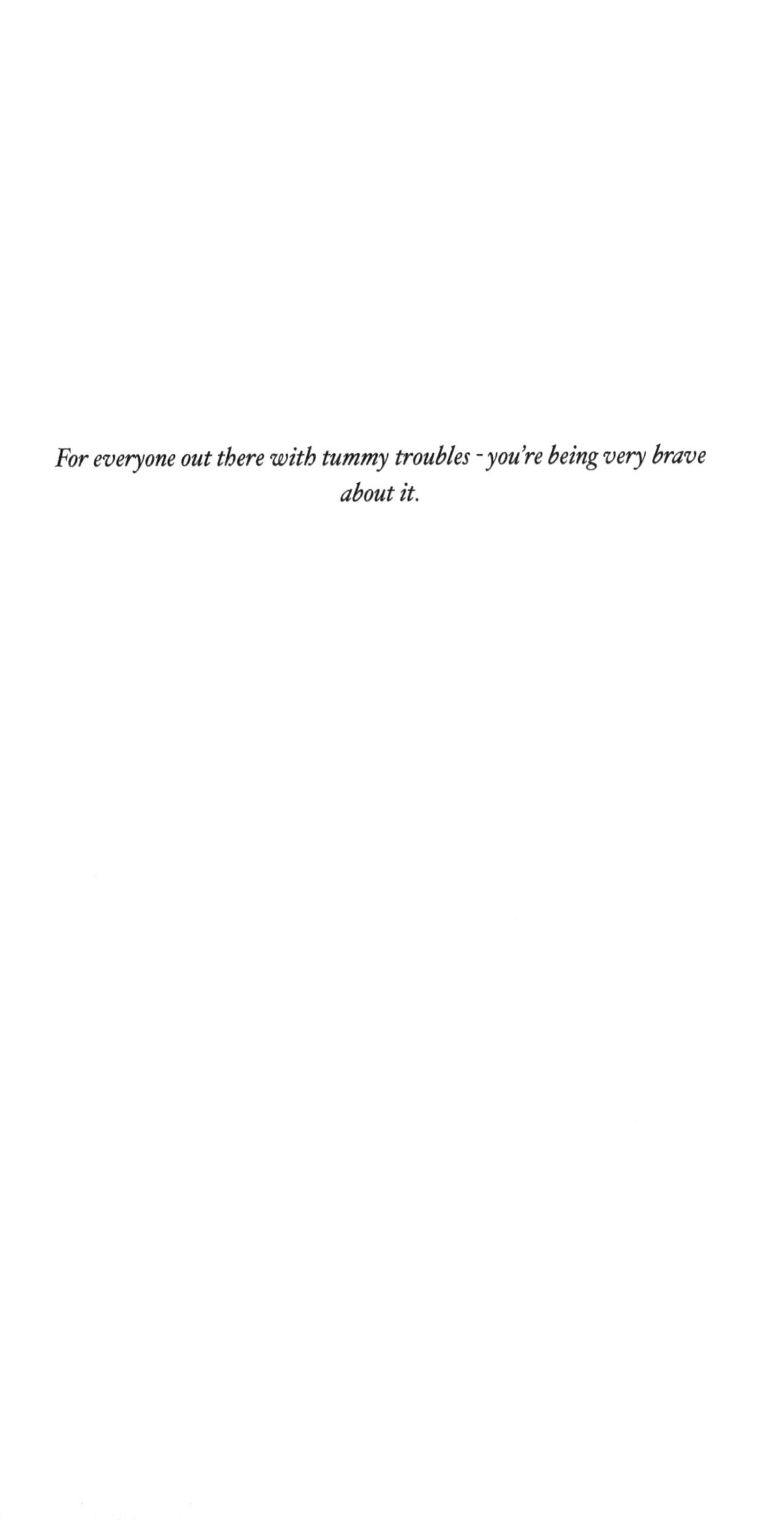

For everyone out there with tummy troubles - you're being very brave about it.

CHAPTER

One

JAX

Norms for everyday life existed most adults were able to adhere to. Not shitting yourself in public was one of them.

But irritable bowel syndrome doesn't always play by normal rules. So, I found myself, once again, desperate to find a bathroom thanks to my current IBS flare up. My stomach rested calmly when I left to walk around the Mall from my Capitol Hill sublet twenty minutes ago. Now trapped in a desert of easy bathroom options, I needed one as desperately as readers need the next book after a cliffhanger.

I wiped sweat off my brow that had no business forming there on a chilly February day and looked around again. On the easternmost side of the Mall sat nothing but congressional office buildings—the Library of Congress, the Supreme Court and, of course, the Capitol itself. Pulling up Google Maps, to see if a secret Starbucks popped up in the past few days, only served to remind me I was about to be up shit creek—literally—without a paddle.

Piles from last week's snowstorm lay parallel to the sidewalks lining the back half of the Capitol between the Capitol building itself and First Street. The dirty, greyish mounds were doubling as guide rails, pointing me toward the steps leading down to the visitor's entrance of the country's legislative seat. With no other choice, I took off at a brisk, but not too brisk, walk.

"I can't fucking believe I'm about to do this," I muttered, removing my gloves so I could run my fingers through my long brown hair where it poked out under a blue beanie. I approached one of the Capitol Police officers by the door, doing my best to look casual and like I had any business approaching the visitor's entrance besides, you know, business.

"Hi there. Is this where the line starts?"

The officer, who looked like he'd rather be anywhere else than outside in the freezing temperatures minding lines of tourists, jerked his head to the area behind me.

"Line starts back there. Lead up to a holiday weekend, lots of tourists in town."

I turned around and saw a large crowd waiting to enter the first screening area to start their Capitol tour.

"Shit," I muttered.

I pivoted back to the man, who seemed desperate to not meet my eyes, as my stomach twinged painfully again. I put on my best I-can-get-you-to-tell-me-anything smile and abandoned the last traces of my dignity. "I just need to duck into the restroom. Any chance I could cut in?"

The man shook his head, dismissing me again, keeping an eye peeled for anything out of the ordinary. Guess the smile fails in effectiveness when it was covering up grimaces and panic.

I nodded and made my way back to the steps, my mind racing for other options.

"Miss?"

I stopped three steps from the bottom and turned.

A different officer stood next to my original not-savior and looked at his colleague. They muttered something to each other and looked back at me.

"Is it an emergency?" Apparently, this new officer overheard our exchange from his post by the door.

"Yes," I said, aware of how desperate I sounded, but not willing to care.

"Come on then," my new best friend said. He waved me down toward the entrance and opened the door so I could scoot on through.

"Thank you so much. I hope you get off door duty soon. Or they invest in heaters for you all or . . . or something."

Chuckling, he waved me on inside, saying, "Good luck," with the inflection and tone of understanding only someone else who suffered from gastrointestinal distress on a regular basis could manage.

I removed my coat and emptied my pockets so I could walk through the metal detector. Once through security, I made my way to the top level of the Capitol Visitors Center. Not unlike any other time I entered a public space, my eyes searched for the signage showing the way to the bathroom. Even though work brought me to the Capitol routinely, being in the visitors center was a rare occasion. Thoughts of my job added an additional ache to my troubles, unrelated to my current bowel workings.

A glorious wall placard showed a women's room available both to my left and to my right. As a left-handed gal, I went with the lucky left side and hurried down the hallway, the side-by-side openings to a set of restrooms coming into focus in front of me. I moved faster, only to come to a sudden stop in the middle of the walkway. There were stanchions drawn across both openings.

So, back in the other direction I went, again cursing the lament of the southpaw. While I moved in active pursuit of finding a bathroom, I felt briefly in control of my body again. Each failure, however, pushed me closer to ruin—ruining these pants. I approached the other set of bathrooms and saw there were stanchions blocking the entrance to these facilities, too.

"What the fuck?" I said out loud, my frustration bubbling

over. A tour guide passing through followed my gaze to the unavailable toilets. "Sorry, ma'am. Something's wrong with the water in this part of the building. It's all shut off. There's a single occupancy bathroom down by the tour start on its own system that's still open. You can head down those stairs—"

Before she had time to finish her directions, I took off toward the stairs she indicated, throwing a quick "thank you" over my shoulder. I set off in pursuit of the one working bathroom available to the whole public right now, hoping I'd get lucky. My feet pounded down the stairs, dodging families and visitors speaking in other languages. My toilet-finding senses kicked in as I hit the solid floor again. I hurried to my right, only to find a fifteen-person queue for the single occupancy bathroom I thought would be my savior.

"Fuck, fuck, fuckity fuck," I said, stomping my foot a bit. I ignored the scandalized looks from Ma and Pop from rural-flyover USA, feeling near tears. Everything in life felt out of my control, including my own body's functions. Why should the availability of bathrooms in one of the most popular tourist attractions in the city be any different? I probably should get out of these hallowed halls before I soiled them more than your average lawmaker did daily.

"Everything okay? Did you miss the start of the pre-tour movie? Someone's standing right inside the door. They'll let you in," a voice said next to me.

I looked up to find a tall, brown-haired man wearing a smile that seemed to be very much of the on-the-clock variety and not genuine. I blinked up at him a few times, trying to clear the moisture from my eyes, but not before his smile quickly twisted into a frown. As my vision cleared, I realized he looked familiar. I think he served on the staff of one of the senators from . . . somewhere in New England. Right now, the mental energy powering my Senate staffer Rolodex was engaged in clenching abdominal muscles.

"Really. Are you okay?"

Maybe his familiarity mixed with how he donned that fake smile again pushed me past a breaking point.

"No. I'm really not okay. I don't have a place to live. I could lose my job any day. It's fucking freezing outside, and *I just need to find a bathroom.*"

This last part came out louder than I meant it to, causing those closest in the cavernous visitors center to turn toward us.

"Well, uh," the man said, glancing around at the attention we were gathering. "I know there's a line for the one over there. But there are a few upstairs, you just take—"

"Nope. They're out of order. Which is just my luck. Okay, well, I'll be seeing you."

"Wait." the man put his hand on my shoulder, which caused me to whirl around—out for blood. My normal disposition bordered on storm cloud more than sunshine, but throw the week I'd had into the mix of my stomach issues and I wouldn't be above seeing heads roll. Starting with this man, no matter how well he might wear that suit.

He put his hands up. "Got it, no touching. I was supposed to be meeting someone for a tour, but they're late anyway. Just, come with me."

The man walked toward a doorway that led out of the visitors center. I stayed still, dumbstruck for a moment that this stranger seemed to want to help me. Maybe his head could stay firmly attached after all. Realizing he might be my best chance at a respectable resolution to this bathroom fiasco, I quickly started moving and caught up to him.

As we dodged the crowds, he pulled a visitor pass out of his jacket pocket and handed it to me. "You're Jacqueline Carter, right? You work for *Politics Daily*? Put this on."

I pulled the lanyard over my head, no time to answer his questions before we reached a security guard positioned at the doorway. My guide smiled and flashed his badge at the waiting guard, pausing at her booth.

The security guard waved her hand, indicating we could walk

through. "You know, Preston, I think you just like showing off how good your picture turned out on the new badges. I know who you are." She smiled good-naturedly.

"It's not my fault I photograph well in artificial lighting," Preston responded, a more authentic smile tipping his lips. "Besides, Bernice, I'm a rule follower. You know that."

"Yeah, yeah. Have a good one. Tell Senator Marsden I said hello." She nodded to me and moved her eyes past us to focus on the next person trying to enter through her doorway.

The professional black book finally kicked in and I realized the man next to me was Preston Brandt, Senator Marsden's Chief of Staff.

"Wait, we're headed to Marsden's office?" I realized Preston intended to take me to their office suite. I hadn't entered any of the Congress staff buildings from the visitors center before. Preston gestured to follow him down the long hallway.

"So, you are Jacqueline then. I recognized you from our conference on abortion access last week. Are you okay with stairs? The tunnel is probably quicker to make it to the Russell Building than a people mover unless we time it exactly right."

"Uh, stairs are fine. And it's Jax. Not Jacqueline." Preston's rapid-fire method of questioning helped keep my mind off the pressing issue that instigated our little field trip.

Preston grabbed the door to his right and held it open for me. As I walked through the doorway, I saw what appeared to be a marble stairwell with a black-iron handrail.

"We're headed down two levels," Preston said, descending. The brisk pace Preston set on the stairs caused my stomach to jostle and returned my attention to the matter at hand. I took a deep breath, my inner monologue repeating, "on our way, on our way," with every step we climbed.

We exited the stairwell to a white hallway. Preston glanced up at the lighted sign indicating the next people mover wouldn't arrive at this stop for another three minutes.

"It's only about a three-minute walk across—okay to keep moving?"

"Flat ground moving is good. Let's go."

We walked past another security guard who greeted my companion in the same congenial way as the first. *Apparently, the Chief of Staff is also a teacher's pet*, I thought, as my stomach twisted painfully.

Things were getting close to emergency status again, but as we turned another corner, a doorway at the end of the hall came into view.

Preston held open the door for me and greeted yet another guard, before directing me with his arm to a stairwell right across from the tunnel entrance.

"Just up another quick flight and we'll be there."

I nodded and ducked through the doorway, the marble stairs and wooden handrail a blur. All my concentration went to clenching and putting one foot in front of the other. We exited into a hallway with black and white tile on the floor and large wooden doors lining each side.

"We're right here." Preston stepped ahead of me to open the door next to the stairwell. As we entered, I read *Senator Mitchell Marsden, Rhode Island*, on a plaque to the right of the solid oak doorframe.

"Our staff bathroom is right through there." Preston pointed to a seating area to the left of the doorway. "My cubicle is the first one on the left down that hallway." He pointed again, this time directly in front of us.

I bolted to the left, getting a thank you out before shutting the door to the bathroom behind me. The situation was the most dire right before relief, as usual.

As I sat there, my hands cradled my head. I couldn't believe I'd followed a staffer into a senator's office for this. It was a top three all-time bathroom desperation story. One I would look forward to telling my gastroenterologist when I had my long-awaited appointment with them next month. I'd let Doc weigh in on if it belonged ahead of or behind when my date left me behind thinking I bailed since I spent so long in the bathroom after we ordered. Joke's on her though. I got to take both entrées home, *and* the waitress comped me a dessert since technically I got ditched.

After a while, it seemed safe to move on, and I looked at myself in the mirror as I washed my hands. Now that the urgency of the situation was behind me, the mirror showed my flushed cheeks redden as I considered facing Preston, unassuming IBS savior of the week. I gathered my coat and bag from where I dropped them on the floor and bit the inside of my cheek. Could I sneak out of here without facing him again? I hadn't been paying super close attention to our journey into the Russell Building, but figured I could find my way out if I needed to.

After I sprayed the low-fragrance air freshener I kept in my bag for such occasions, I looked down at the visitor badge around my neck. My other badge seemed to glow brightly from where it sat buried deep in my bag. I wasn't even sure I could leave the building as a visitor without my escort, and the badge in my bag would get me out of here through a different entrance, no problem. Though, since I technically didn't have an active contract, I was positive if my boss found out I used it, I could kiss that contract renewal goodbye.

The door to the offices slammed against the wall like someone had pushed it open with all their strength. I jumped, wondering who would have the balls to enter a senator's office that way.

"Fucking nosy people and their questions." A man's voice filtered through the closed door to the bathroom. "I want a moratorium on unvetted people in this office for the next week. Or until Warfield Pippen from the House fucks up again. Anyone responsible for another soul in this office who isn't a spouse or a blood relative is done. Make sure to tell the fucking interns." The voice got closer. "Brandt, we're going to need to revisit that speech. Politico published another hit piece, and it's blowing up big time."

My eyes widened as I realized that voice belonged to Senator Marsden. In my current job, I covered the House, so was all too familiar with Pippen and his fuck-ups, as well as his continuous feud with the first-term senator from his state. Now that Pippen was running for the senator nomination for the opposite party in the upcoming election, things had reached a new level of nuclear between them. I nervously reached up to straighten my hair and hat, wondering how I could sneak out of this bathroom. I definitely counted as an unvetted intruder in the office, and, at least for now, also a political reporter. That could be disastrous for Preston.

Footsteps approached the door where I hid in haste. "Wait," a voice I recognized as Preston's called. It sounded like he cut in front of his boss, blocking his access to the bathroom. I could detect a tinge of panic in his voice, even from that one word.

"What, Brandt? I need to piss," Mitchell snapped.

"Uh, we need more toilet paper."

My eyes shifted to the full roll on the dispenser. Preston intended to come in to replace the toilet paper and would come out with a human?

"Pretty sure a shake or two, and I'm fine. But your delicate sensitivities are noted," he said. I didn't hear anyone walking away from the bathroom. Preston must still be standing guard, but for how long?

"And uh, there's someone in there," Preston said, sounding like *he* was going to be the one needing an emergency bathroom trip next.

"What?" the senator asked. His tone portrayed pure ice.

"Uh, give me a second." A knock on the door came next. "Everything okay in there?"

I took a deep breath, unlocked the door, and opened it. Preston stood right in front of me. His eyes were wide, and his cheeks painted with a faint flush. I'd bet money—I didn't have—that if he didn't have a jacket on, I'd see pit stains.

"Follow my lead, okay?" he muttered, holding his hand out to me. Not seeing how I had any other choice, I took a deep breath and put my hand in his. Preston turned around to face the senator.

"Who the fuck is this, Brandt?"

"Senator Marsden, please meet my fiancée."

CHAPTER

Two

PRESTON

Jax tensed under my hand that found its way around her waist while I delivered a boldfaced lie to my boss. I reached for her instinctively and found myself relieved she didn't balk at my touch the way she had in the visitors center. Beads of sweat dripped down my back as I glanced her way. Relief flooded my system to see an expression that displayed no signs of surprise at my declaration. Mitchell did not respond as graciously.

"Your fiancée? I've never seen you bring a partner around anywhere. I honestly thought you might be . . ." Jax winced next to me. "Ace or aromantic or something."

"I just try to keep my personal life separate from my work life," I answered. Not that there had been much personal life to speak of for the past several years. But to pull this off, he definitely didn't need to know that.

This one exchange exemplified the man I had hooked my professional wagon to. He held very progressive and inclusive views, with absolutely no filter. I imagined Jax flinched because she assumed his next word would infer I was gay. Nope, no homophobia here, just a lack of tact that you still shouldn't speculate, especially out loud, about someone's orientation from their lack of significant others. At least we were in our offices this time, but the woman next to me was a reporter, after all.

"That's usually my rule too, but Preston here makes breaking all my rules worthwhile. Jacqueline Carter, it's nice to meet you, Senator." Jacqueline for my boss, but Jax for me. I didn't know what to make of the disparity, let alone the enthusiasm with which she was selling our situation. Senator Marsden returned her shake half-heartedly before pulling out his phone.

"Hmm," the senator said, only half participating in a conversation he started. Another winning quality we hadn't been able to break him of. "You work in politics too?" His disinterest was clear.

"Something like that," Jax answered in a cool tone that seemed to display she too found the senator's affect toward other humans unimpressive.

"Well, it's nice to meet you. I assume we'll be seeing you at the fundraising dinner tomorrow night?"

"Oh, well, I didn't let Laurel know I'd be bringing a plus-one, so I'm sure the seating chart is—"

"Laurel?" the senator bellowed, not looking up from his phone.

Laurel came around the corner a moment later. "Yes, Senator Marsden?"

Her face took on a neutral and placid expression. I knew from a drunken night during our fourth year that meant she was envisioning leaving him stranded at the airport without a ride scheduled and his phone dead. Too bad being a general asshole wasn't enough of a reason to sabotage yourself and get fired. Plus, he got shit done.

"Make sure Preston has an extra seat at his table tomorrow night for his woman here." The senator gestured in Jax's general direction with his phone, not bothering to meet Laurel's eyes. That worked in my favor because those eyes widened in shock at the sight of a woman at my side in our offices *and* at the declaration that she belonged to me. Laurel had, as recently as last week, been trying to convince me to go on a blind date with some cousin of hers.

"No problem. I can shuffle a few things around." She looked between Jax and me, clearly trying to figure out what she missed.

"Great. Preston, I'll email you about the speech updates. If you can, draft a press release response too."

"You know, if we hired one of those Communication Director candidates you interviewed last month, they would already have something drafted for you to review . . ." I said, trying to keep my tone even, but I sensed a migraine coming on.

"Yeah, yeah, we'll get to it. In the meantime, you've got it. You already write speeches, just write something for the press. Easy, right? Okay, I'm off to play squash with Senator Craft. Grease some wheels for that voting rights legislation and shit. Later."

And with that, my boss turned on his heel, maneuvered around Laurel, who still stood behind him in the hallway. She, Jax, and I waited in silence until we heard the outer door shut again.

I massaged my forehead with my fingers at the bridge of my nose. "Shall we move this into the conference room, ladies?" I gestured with my arm for Jax to follow Laurel back down the hallway, avoiding the eyes of the other staffers following us curiously.

The descent into one of the swivel chairs around the table was more plop than sit. I found myself exhausted, with at least another eight hours left in this day, thanks to the press release the senator just threw onto my plate.

"So, that was Senator Marsden? I would be offended he didn't remember me since I asked him the question about abortion rights last week that went viral, but it seems he would forget his own mother's birthday," Jax said, crossing her arms in front of her.

"As the person who sends his mother's birthday presents, I can confirm," Laurel said, laughing. She faced me and said, "I like her. But, pray tell, when the fuck did you have time to find a fiancée?" She threw herself down in one of the rolling chairs around the conference table, her face incredulous.

"Where's the Tylenol?" I ignored her accurate and pointed barb about the lack of romance in my life as I massaged my temples, which unsurprisingly were pounding.

"Are you feeling better, Jax?" I asked, cringing immediately. God, I hoped Senator Marsden's lack of filter wasn't finally wearing off on me.

Jax laughed. "Yes, much. Thank you. The panic is almost as bad as the act itself, if you're asking me. Though, I have to say, my IBS panic has never landed me a fiancé before. There's a first time for everything." Digging into her bag, Jax retrieved a bottle of painkillers, shaking it in my direction as if to ask a question.

Popping the pills into my mouth, I swallowed them dry before responding. "Sorry about the fiancée thing. I panicked when I heard him come in raging about unvetted people."

"So, in your panic, you went to fiancée? What about sister, cousin, AA sponsor, Girl Scout cookie supplier . . . anything else?" Laurel asked from her slumped position, laughing at my pain.

"Your observation is both . . . helpful and astute as always." Sarcasm bled through my tone.

Laurel stopped laughing for a moment. "So, do I actually need to add a seat at our table for tomorrow or . . ."

"No, definitely not. I'll figure something—"

"Now, wait just a minute," Jax interjected. "I know I'm new here, but *that* does not seem like a man who would take very kindly to a direct order being ignored. What happens if you show up without a fiancée to this fundraiser tomorrow? Won't he wonder who I actually am?"

"She has a point," Laurel added, her face entirely too gleeful at the sticky situation I found myself in. *I'll be hearing about this for weeks.*

"I could do it. I could be your fiancée," Jax declared, nodding as if she had decided something.

I groaned.

"Okay, I cannot even begin to unpack that statement or what would be in it for you. I need to apparently rewrite a speech and now draft a press release, too. I'll be here until seven at least."

"Well, you need to eat, right? Let's meet for dinner tonight. Le Dip sound okay? We can talk about it all then."

"Okay, fine. I'll see you then," I agreed, surprising myself. Why did I feel the need to continue contact with this woman? We can't actually be engaged. Beyond her employer, I knew absolutely nothing about her. Laurel had a point. I really didn't have time to date anyone. Nonetheless, I was planning to meet an almost stranger for dinner.

"Well, then," Laurel said, pushing herself to her feet, sounding thrilled with the development. "I'm off to find one Miss Jax a seat at our table. I'm assuming you have a last name to go with that on the table card?"

"I'll fill you in on my way out. Can I get out by myself or do I need an escort?"

I shook my head.

"If you go down the stairwell we came up, you'll eventually hit an exit onto Constitution."

"Well then, until tonight. Have a great day at the office, schnookums."

Laurel shot me a smirk over her shoulder, her eyes sparkling with the promise of the third degree later on as the women exited the conference room, chattering on their way back to Laurel's desk and the exit. Laurel kept just as busy as me, but managed to move in with her girlfriend last year. My reticence to dating went deeper than my busy schedule.

I rubbed my eyes hard, wondering if, when I opened them, the last hour would all be a dream. I could not have a fake fiancée. The idea was ridiculous and something out of the books my stepmother, Margaret, read. This was not real life. I resolved

I would be firm with Jax as soon as I got to Le Diplomate tonight. At the same time, she had a point. I needed to eat. It would be good for me to have a hard stop and a reason to leave the office tonight. Seven often turned into nine, ten, eleven before I could drag myself back to my apartment.

I shook my head to clear it and forced myself to sink into ultra-focused mode, where nothing existed outside of work.

As the rest of the world disappeared, a voice inside me whispered. It wondered if I had spent too much time ignoring anything outside my job recently, and if Jax dropping into my life could be a sign.

CHAPTER
Three

JAX

I turned the key to enter the front door of a row house on New Jersey Avenue. The building I could lay claim to for another twenty-four hours had a bright blue exterior. It coordinated well with the reds and yellows that popped up along the street, interspersed with brick and more neutral colors. I dragged my feet up the two flights of stairs to the top level and used two more keys to unlock the knob and deadbolt before entering the converted two-bedroom I had been subletting for the past six months.

"Ah, Jacqueline, you're back." Estonia, my soon-to-be-ex roommate, breezed into the common areas with an air of contempt. I never made a habit of growing close to my temporary roommates, knowing we'd part sooner rather than later, but Estonia counted as the first time a living situation turned antagonistic. She claimed to not be biphobic, but her attitude toward me changed when I brought a guy home the Wednesday before Thanksgiving, after bringing home a sexy lady nurse on Halloween. Since then, the air in the apartment had been chilly, no matter how high she cranked the thermostat. "I noticed that Lyric's room is still full of your belongings. You know that—"

"Yes, I know. I need to have everything out by 11:59 p.m.

tomorrow, because beloved Lyric is returning bright and early Saturday morning. It'll all be gone." Where it would be gone *to* was still up in the air. I removed my phone from the pocket of my parka to see if anyone on the couch-surfing site had responded to my ad requesting space for the next week. A depressing lack of notifications from that app were displayed on my screen. Instead, a badge displaying an email from my boss, Mark Hertzog, had appeared since I last checked.

"Well, if that's all," I said, turning my back on Estonia and shutting my door, not bothering to listen to what she was saying as the piece of wood met the frame. Apparently, she had more things to say, but I couldn't bring myself to care as I opened the email, my hands shaking. It was a message telling me to report to the office tomorrow, right? If I had a paycheck again, I could always get a hotel or Airbnb for a few days.

My contract expired last week, and while all signs seemed to indicate it would be renewed, negotiations *coincidentally* ground to a halt when my romance author pen name was connected with my real-world identity. I still wasn't sure how Peggy Rappencourt, over at *The Washington Dispatch*, had figured it out. Perhaps my baiting of her in my series of articles on women's rights and her antiquated views might have something to do with her motivation. Why spend your time researching your position when repeating versions of the same lines resonated so strongly with your base? Better to take your rival down instead. Something archaic about a steamy romance novelist not being able to be nuanced on family values was the position *The Dispatch* had taken, threatening to go public. I hadn't disclosed my pen name when I got hired for this job last year. While I knew Mark thought their positions were outdated and, frankly, misogynistic, that didn't mean he needed to stick his neck out for a freelancer whose contract had a convenient expiration date.

I took in the words displayed on my phone, sinking down onto my bed. My contract would not be renewed. In my file, they'd phrased it as downsizing, which happened more often than not in today's news world. There wouldn't be a black mark on my record this way, and I could use him as a reference. Ironic how the job I wished I could do full time ended up costing me the job I took so I could make ends meet while I worked on my next series.

I threw my phone face down on the bed and my body followed its path, lying down on the purple and white quilt my grandma made for me when I was born, parka and all. I lay there, like a puffy starfish, staring at my ceiling, wondering what in the world I would do. The balance of my bank account read alarmingly low. Couch-surfing sites only took payment via cash, directly to said couch owner. My credit card still had some space on it, but I needed to eat too.

At the word eat, I could almost hear the metaphorical light-bulb click on over my head. I hadn't been entirely sure why I insisted Preston and I schedule dinner for tonight after our run-in. Sure, a sense of owing him something for acting as savior and facing an awkward situation with his boss was part of it. But I didn't expect him to want to keep up our engagement charade. A memory from Preston's conversation with the senator before he left their offices flickered through my mind. The stress that showed in Preston's face and shoulders with having to draft a press release along with rewriting a speech had been palpable. If he agreed to my plan, the space two meals and probably lots of alcohol would take toward my credit limit may prove well worth it.

I sat in a cream cushioned booth in the garden room at Le Diplomate, nursing a glass of red wine. The maître d' would direct Preston to the table when he arrived. I arrived twenty minutes early, wanting to be already situated as my dinner date approached, locking in for my own sake that I was in charge here. Preston was now fifteen minutes late, and my stomach churned with the oaky liquid at the idea he might not show. The neighboring tables seemed too close, the chattering of my neighbors closing in on our small two-top table. I would have killed for one of their infamous booths, but I was already going to serve as fact checker to an old colleague for a month to repay them for getting me a reservation at all. Beggars can't be choosers.

I toyed with my fork, questioning the sanity of an idea which seemed so genius in the light of day. As my neighbor discussed their ingrown toenail removal surgery, I wondered what they would make of two people hammering out a fake engagement arrangement. If Preston bothered to show, that is.

The scent of laundry and fresh mint filled my nose, rising above the rich scents of herbs and freshly baked bread. I tilted my head to see Preston standing next to our table. His hands were jammed in his pockets as he gazed down at me, his expression impossible to read.

"Don't tell me you're one of those people who believes eating standing up is better for digestion." I smiled, hoping he found my snark charming.

"I'm still not sure why I'm here. If I don't sit, it makes bailing a lot easier."

Across from me, I pushed the chair back with my foot, issuing a clear invitation. I hoped he'd make the decision to stay.

"You're here because even Chiefs of Staff for asshole senators, who happen to have one of the most progressive voting records in recent memory and an uncanny knack for getting his bills to the floor for a first-term national politician, need to eat."

Preston maneuvered himself into the chair and pulled up close to the table.

"Sounds like someone had a busy afternoon," he muttered, unrolling his silverware and putting the napkin on his lap. I reached to pour him some wine out of the bottle that had been breathing on our table.

"I don't get a choice of drink?"

"I'll get you something else if you want it, but this bottle came highly recommended by our waiter and even more highly priced, so I promise it'll go down easy."

Preston picked up his glass, swirling the contents once, and lifted it to his lips for a sip. He considered the pallet after swallowing, setting the glass back down.

"Okay, that'll do."

I considered him for a moment. While being a reporter wasn't my first choice of careers, I had a knack for reading people that came in handy while sniffing out a story, or more often, picking up on bullshit.

"You don't know shit about wine, do you?"

Preston's cheeks reddened slightly, before he speared me with an assessing gaze of his own.

"Okay, no. I usually buy whatever is right around the ten-dollar a bottle range. But let me guess, you're an eight-dollar bottle girl."

I laughed. "Like I said, the waiter recommended it, and I didn't ask any questions. His accent intimidated me."

Preston laughed too, picking up his glass and took a more generous sip.

"It's clear we've both got this reading-other-people thing down, so let's save some time and just be honest with each other tonight, okay?"

Preston nodded. He looked a bit wary, but I appreciated his willingness to agree to be open with me from the get go.

The waiter walked up just then.

"Now that your other party is here, do you have any questions about the menu? Or have you decided on a starter?"

"You got any food allergies or sensitivities, Brandt?"

Preston shook his head.

"Up for an adventure?" I held my breath while I waited for his answer. His willingness to trust me to order for him was a low-stakes test for what I had planned.

He shrugged in response before nodding slowly. I could work with that.

"We'll take the chef's special—appetizer, entrée, and dessert." I hoped the hit to my credit card and the risk to my stomach would be worth it by the end of the night. Oftentimes, even though the food was richer, the lack of processed ingredients in restaurants like this could play nice with my digestive system.

"I actually studied abroad in France while I was in college," Preston said, breaking the silence that fell across the table after the waiter left. He leaned forward to grab a piece of bread out of the basket another waiter smoothly dropped off without even breaking his stride.

"See, look. There's something about you I didn't learn this afternoon in my research. And to think, they say couples stop surprising each other eventually." I poked around the fiancé issue to see how Preston would react.

"Yeah, about that," Preston said, not looking up from buttering his roll. "I'll just tell Senator Marsden you got a job offer, had to move, and we're doing long distance. It's a reelection year, my schedule was too hard for you, we break up eventually, and it's all over."

I took in a deep breath. I just need to keep him in his seat after this next part, and I might have a fighting chance. "And what if we didn't do that?"

"Didn't tell him we broke up?" Preston held his freshly buttered bread inches from his mouth.

"Didn't break up at all."

CHAPTER
Four

PRESTON

I'd heard the term hysterical laughter before, but never experienced it firsthand. Our neighbors were staring, I could feel it, but still my shoulders shook, my eyes teared, and noise continued to leave my mouth. I hadn't slept more than five hours a night over the past week, and once I got started, I couldn't stop.

Jax did her best to ignore my outburst, pouring herself a fresh glass of wine. I slowly got myself under control, wiping under my eyes with my napkin before setting it back in my lap.

"Okay, okay, I'm sorry. I think I must be extra sleep deprived today. You said we shouldn't break up like you thought we should stay fake engaged and I lost it." A few stray chuckles slipped out. What an incredulous thing to say.

Jax shrugged as she took a sip of her wine. "I do mean I think we should stay fake engaged. We both have things we need, and I think we can help each other."

My eyes widened as I started to believe her. She really wasn't kidding. "I barely know anything about you, other than you're a political reporter and, well, that you have IBS. I'm not sure how that translates into grounds for a relationship."

"Well," Jax said. "For starters, you're right. Giving the chef free rein over my food choices tonight may cause hellfire to rain down later, but at least I'll be at home with my own toilet. And I, as you may have figured out, don't believe in sugarcoating my body's malfunctions for the sake of other's delicate constitutions. Second, in full transparency, my living situation is in flux, so moving in with a fiancé would really help me out of a jam."

"Moving in?" I spluttered the sip of wine I had just taken.

Jax waved her hand, as if suggesting I release the thought from my mind. "We'll come back to that. Third, I'm not a political reporter anymore. My contract expired and I found out today they're not going to renew it."

"Shit, I'm sor—"

Jax waved me off. "Don't be. I've been writing in the political realm for the last five years after getting my MFA. It started with local politics and I worked my way up to the big stage. That's not because I love it, but because the best man at my parent's wedding gave me a job out of pity five years ago when I was desperate. I've hopped from publication to publication since then. And today, I decided to stop hopping."

Our conversation paused as the waiter delivered our appetizers, Steak Tartare du Parc. Jax and I dug into the food, which smelled amazing.

After a few minutes of plating our food and murmurs over the delicious taste, Jax rolled her shoulders and started her pitch.

"I couldn't help but hearing your office needs some comms help?"

"This is off the record?"

"My god, there's no record for it to be on! But yes, sure, it's off the record."

I sighed. "Yes, we need comms help. Our former Communications Director got allocated to the staff for the campaign, and I can't get Senator Marsden to replace one for our office. I'm already writing speeches for both his campaign and appearances for his current term because he won't take speeches from anyone else. Now he's making me write press releases and handle inter-view requests too, on top of managing the rest of the staff. I'm going to die from an ulcer before I ever get to run for office myself."

Jax smiled like a cat who finally caught that pesky canary.

"I had you pegged for personal political aspirations. Why else would you put up with that bastard?"

"He's not that bad . . ." I trailed off, looking to either side of our table to be sure our dinner mates were engaged in conversa-tion before leaning closer. "Okay, he *is* that bad. But he does a lot of good work for causes I'm passionate about, and I started as Chief of Staff for a senator when I was only twenty-eight. I couldn't pass up that kind of job offer."

"I totally understand doing what you need to do to achieve your goals—which is where I come in."

Jax and I stared at each other as they cleared our appetizer and placed our entrée of Porc Milanese in front of us.

"Monsieur and madame, anything else you need right now?"

"We're all set for now, thank you," Jax answered, never breaking her gaze from mine.

I picked up my knife and fork, cutting into my dinner. I meant to tell Jax to save it, I wasn't interested, but I heard myself, as if from an out-of-body experience, saying, "Okay, I'm listening."

"So, let me see if I have this straight," I said to the gorgeous woman across from me, setting my silverware down on my empty plate. Throughout our courses, it occurred to me she might be an evil mastermind. "We continue to pretend we're engaged. To sell that ruse, you move in with me and we act like a couple in front of family, friends, and colleagues. In return, you'll take the Comms Director role in the senator's office, so I don't have to continue to do two jobs and die an early death."

"Don't forget you won't have to admit to the senator you lied to him, and it'll be a good look for you to have a committed partner as you explore launching your own campaign in a year or two. Probably eighteen months, right? House of Representatives?"

I felt my jaw drop open. I hadn't even told any of my brothers I planned to run for the House in the next election cycle.

"I thought you said you weren't good at this political reporter thing."

Jax dabbed her mouth with her napkin. "I said I didn't want the job to begin with. Not that I wasn't great at it." She looked around for our waiter. "Do you think we need a nightcap to go with our dessert, to officially toast our engagement? Maybe a glass of port?"

"I don't think I've ever actually had port. I usually have to run out and do something for Mitchell when it gets to that part of the evening."

"Port, it is." She made eye contact with our waiter. After confirming it would go well with whatever dessert masterpiece they'll be bringing out momentarily, she put in the order.

As the waiter walked away again, I asked, "So, if you didn't want to be a political reporter, what was your focus for your MFA program?"

"Ah, you have found the line of honesty the evening doesn't extend past," Jax answered, picking up her glass and swallowing the last swig of her wine. Her eyes clouded. It seemed this woman could see through most of my secrets and pick out needs I couldn't voice out loud, but was determined to hold some things close to the chest. My mind flickered back to my last relationship. Maybe there were some areas where I should do the same.

Before I could push any further about Jax's writing aspirations, our waiter returned with two glasses of port and a single plate. The dish held a delicious mountain of chocolate confection and two forks.

"How precious, jelly bean," Jax teased. "Should I feed you from my fork, or do you want to feed me first?"

"How about we just keep to our own forks," I said, my face heating for the umpteenth time this evening.

Jax shrugged, speared the pastry with her fork, and brought a dessert the restaurant could rename "death by chocolate" to her lips. As the bite settled on her tongue, her eyes closed and she let out a moan entirely indecent for the public setting we were in. I found myself shocked to wonder how I could get her to make that noise again. It hadn't escaped my notice that Jax was gorgeous, with her fringe bangs dusting her eyebrows and her blue eyes piercing me with each question she asked or point she made. Danger lay in finding your potential fake fiancée attractive.

"Shall we toast?" Jax asked, lifting her glass, effectively breaking me out of my reverie.

I lifted mine in answer, not for the first time that evening admiring how her eyes sparkled in the candlelight. We made a far-fetched and ridiculous pair, but I couldn't deny Jax represented a solution to my work problems. Something in me felt called to her. My brothers always teased me for collecting strays growing up, delivering them to the no-kill shelter in our town or nursing baby birds back to health that had fallen from their nests. Jax stroked those same instincts.

"To our happily ever after?" I offered, trying to get into the spirit of our sham betrothal, bringing my glass to meet hers.

A look of sorrow and shame crossed Jax's face for an instant, mirroring misgivings I tried to bury deep inside myself. In the next moment, she smiled at me and brought her glass to her lips. She finished the toast. "Certainly to our happily for now."

The delivery of the check brought a slight squabble over who would pay the bill. Jax won handily. "You agreed to marry me tonight. The least I can do is buy you dinner."

Now we were standing outside waiting on the curb for our respective rides.

"So, I'll bring my stuff to your place tomorrow, early afternoon, so we can arrive at the fundraiser together?" Jax's eyes were on her phone, presumably tracking the location of her ride share, showing no sign of the bombshell she just dropped on me.

"To-tomorrow? I mean, I'm not sure—"

"I had a male roommate in grad school. Nothing about the state of your place can faze me."

"Oh, it's not that. I'm actually very clean and neat . . ."

Jax dragged her eyes slowly up and down my frame, her gaze like a tangible weight. Like she could see directly through the wool peacoat I donned against the chill.

"I can see that," she responded when she had finished her perusal. What did *that* mean?

"If you're done," I huffed. "It's just that I don't know if I can meet you tomorrow. The senator and I have to go over his speech and then I should work on the press and comms stuff."

Jax shook her head. "I'm going to help you with that, remember? We can spend time on it Saturday, pro bono really, since I won't even be on the payroll yet. You can't tell me you're not the type to work on weekends. And if I move in tomorrow, then we won't even have to leave the house to work."

As I thought this over, Jax plucked my phone out of my hand. She held it up to my face to unlock it and then opened up a text message thread. After hitting send, her phone vibrated in her other hand, ensuring I had my new fiancée's phone number.

"Here's your car." Jax nodded toward the car pulling to the curb, handing my phone back. "Text me your address. I'll plan to be there around two. I don't have much stuff. We can get it unloaded in your guest room and have plenty of time to get ready before dinner."

"Guest room? Oh, I don't have a—"

The car honked its horn, cutting me off.

"Your car is going to leave if you don't get in."

"Is your ride almost here? I can tell him to wait."

Jax waved me off. "He'll be here in a minute. He's just turning the corner."

We were on a well-lit street, and I needed to get home so I could make sure my apartment was in shape to receive another person's belongings in less than eighteen hours.

"Okay, well, I guess I'll see you tomorrow?" I stood there awkwardly, not sure how to say goodbye to the woman planning to move in with me.

My driver honked again, breaking up the awkward moment.

Jax laughed. "Go. We'll work on physical touch tomorrow."

I opened the back door, slid into the car, and shut the door behind me. What Jax meant by "working on physical touch" clicked as the car pulled away from the curb. I wheeled my head around in time to see Jax set off in the opposite direction. No cars stopped to pick her up. I settled into the seat as the driver merged into traffic, running my hand through my hair. This morning, my most intimate relationship was with my doorman. Now, I had an impending roommate, and more alarmingly, a fake fiancée, plus a potential solution to one of my future work-related ulcers, all in one Jax-shaped package. Who exactly was this brunette sorceress who had dropped into my life?

CHAPTER
Five

JAX

It turned out Preston's apartment building was only a few blocks away from my sublet in Capitol Hill. I could tell the short distance confused my rideshare driver, but he gamely loaded up my few boxes and bags anyway, chattering away over the brief route. My stomach was in knots, so I tuned him out. I had concocted some outlandish plans to keep a roof over my head the past few years, but this one may take the prize for most rash. I hadn't even asked if I'd have my own bathroom at Preston's place, something typically at the top of my list of questions. After arriving, I stood on the curb, watching the driver unload my earthly possessions on the curb. I started to wonder exactly how I would get it all inside without being in anyone's way when—

"This is everything?"

I turned around to find Preston standing on the sidewalk with the handle of the luggage cart, like you would find at a hotel, in his hand. The afternoon sun revealed natural highlights in his chestnut brown strands. His frame was naturally lean, but when he leaned down to grab a box and place it on the cart, his shirt stretched tight, revealing toned muscles underneath.

"You're here," I said dumbly, as Preston moved another box onto the cart.

"Well, of course," he said with a smile in the direction of the street as my driver shut the backdoor of his SUV with a thunk. "It's not every day my fiancée moves in." He directed his attention to the driver behind me. "Thanks for delivering her and her stuff in one piece."

The driver nodded and waved, heading off to pick up his next passenger. I looked back at Preston, dumbstruck by his familiar and outward display of our *fake* relationship. I half expected him to call the whole thing off as I finished packing up my boxes this morning. His agreement felt reluctant at best last night. But every time guilt started to creep in, I thought about my dwindling bank account and resolved to make the best of it.

"Just practicing," he said with a smile, loading the last of the boxes and bags onto the cart. "But seriously, is this it? Or will we need to make another trip later?"

I snapped out of it. It was good Preston wasn't treating me like a coiled snake ready to strike, if we were ever going to pull this facade off.

"Nope, this is everything. I haven't had a permanent address in over five years. The amount actually gets smaller and smaller with each move. Hope Lyric enjoys the crust of bread I shoved under her bed as I was leaving this morning." For being out of the country, Lyric had managed to get on my bad side, micromanaging my treatment of her room through Estonia. Catty was not always my first nature, but fake, judgy mean girls brought out the worst in me. It might be nice having a male roommate for a while.

Preston pushed the cart toward the door of his apartment building, waving a fob while pressing a button, so the doors swung open automatically.

"I have keys and a fob for you upstairs," Preston said as we moved through the lobby. He waved at the concierge behind the desk, heading toward the elevator and pushing the button to call the car. "I convinced them to give me a second fob for three months without adding you to the lease. We never talked about how long . . ."

"Three months seems like a good start. I don't know what disgusting habits you engage in within the privacy of your own home yet. We may have to break up because of them."

The doors to the elevators slid open and Preston wheeled the cart in, leaving a small space for me to squeeze between the side of the car and the cart. The age of the building meant the elevators were smaller than modern-day sizes, and I was forced right into Preston's space.

Preston's eyes met mine, his eyes darkening as they held my gaze. "Six," he said in a husky tone.

"I'm sorry?" I said, wondering if he meant to counter for a six-month agreement for our fake engagement. I used a trial-size bottle of a designer shampoo I swiped from Estonia's pile of mail in the living room last night, maybe the scent held more power in the wooing department than I expected.

Preston cleared his throat. "We're headed to floor six. Can you hit the button?" He gestured to the button panel behind me with his chin.

Of course, get in elevator, hit floor number, *then* elevator moves. Maybe the shampoo scent was having negative effects on me, instead of positive effects on anyone around me. I whirled around, smacking my elbow off the wall and finally managed to hit the button for floor six. The old elevator whirred to life, slowly lifting us into the air. The air around me thrummed with Preston's proximity to my back. I was aware of the heat wafting off his body reaching my senses. I shivered, turning the motion into a larger body movement by adjusting the laptop bag slung over my body. Hopefully Preston bought it. The elevator dinged, and the doors opened on floor six. I exited, grateful to put some space between us.

We walked a short way down the hall and Preston unlocked the door to apartment 624. Pushing open the door, he gestured for me to enter, and I did, swiveling my head from left to right to take in my new surroundings. On the left, I found a bed tucked into the corner, an open backed shelving unit separating the bed from the couch. I continued my perusal, seeing a single doorway off to the right.

"Want to keep going so I can get this cart in behind you?" Preston asked. He and all my belongings were still half in the hallway. Taking a few more steps into the apartment, I moved toward the edge of the wall next to the entrance. I curled my head around the corner and found a small kitchen located on the other side.

"Where's the rest of it?" I asked slowly, my brain not wanting to transmit the obvious answer.

"The rest of what? Your stuff's all right here?" He gestured to the cart.

"That door way leads to . . ." I pointed at the door I had spotted on my way in.

"That's the bathroom. There's a closet back by the front door."

"So, you live in a studio," I said, sitting down on a couch that definitely looked more comfortable than it was.

"Yup," Preston said, tucking his hands into his jean front pockets and tilting his chin up. "That a problem?"

"I just never expected . . ."

Preston shrugged. "You know how rent prices are in DC. I'm barely ever here. Either living in the office or traveling back to Rhode Island with the senator, so it didn't make sense to waste money on more space than what I needed for just me. Any extra money gets put away in savings for when . . ."

"For when you run for Congress." I finished for him. This sound decision-making lined up with what I'd learned about Preston so far.

I glanced around more, noting the touches Preston had made to make the space feel homey and welcoming. The complete opposite of how his sterile office had been. There were books about politics and history on the shelves next to me with a few spy thrillers interspersed. Photos of a group of men, at various ages of life, lined the top of the shelves. I assumed these were the brothers Preston had mentioned. Photographs of DC hung on the walls, and I noticed the colorful carpet at my feet.

"You're sure a partner never lived here?" I said, gesturing at the bright and personal touches. "Not that a man can't have good decorating taste, but I've seen your office."

Preston's cheeks reddened. "My stepmother made me breathe some life into the place when it still looked like a sample unit after I'd been here a year. Or else, yeah, it'd look a lot like my office. It does make it more attractive to come home, I have to admit."

Okay. Only one room. Only one bed. Definitely two humans. But, it's a place to live and a job and maybe, just maybe, the opportunity to not feel so fucking alone for once. You can do this, J.

"Okay," I said brightly. "This will work! Good thing I pack light."

Preston laughed. "That does have its advantages. I made some room in the closet for you, and the bottom drawer of the dresser is empty. I also cleared some counter space in the bathroom. We can think of other options if you need more . . ."

I was touched he had taken the time to make space for me in his already cramped quarters. After slotting into other people's homes and lives as a subletter for so long, I expected more of the same.

"I think that'll be a great start. We can go from there."

"Okay, cool. Do you need any help or . . ."

It was my turn to laugh.

"I'm pretty sure we'd trample each other if you tried to help. Do you need to go back to the office or . . ."

Preston shook his head. "No, I'm going to work from the couch for a little bit until we have to start getting ready for the gala. I'll just put my headphones on and zone out. Leave you to it."

I shrugged and turned to the cart to grab the first box off the top of my stack. I figured all my movement would be pretty distracting, but Preston was a big boy who could make his own decisions. I set to work layering my clothes into my new drawer, using hangers to hang what I could in the closet and lining my shoes next to Preston's on the floor of the closet. My things had never shared space so intimately with someone else's and it made me almost itchy. Keeping my guard up around Preston in these tight quarters would be tricky, but if he worked as much as he said he did, we should get some separation.

Except that you're working with him now too, numbnuts. You better hope this doesn't backfire.

I flitted around the apartment, finding space here and there for the few knickknacks and personal items I allowed myself to keep move after move. My shampoo bottles sat next to his in the shower, and I shoved tampons under the sink. I smiled to myself. Nothing said cohabiting like introducing feminine products into a man's cabinet.

Soon all my stuff was squared away. Preston's place embodied the minimalist lifestyle, which gave me room to squeeze in around the edges. A pile of things I kept on a bedside table was on the foot of the bed, including my grandmother's quilt. I paused looking at the stark white duvet covering the mattress. We could brighten the bed up with my quilt. Or it could become a couch blanket for a little while. Needing to sit on the couch to snuggle with my quilt could give me the incentive I needed to ever sit on the damn thing, as I remembered the lumps I felt earlier. What I really needed to know was which side of the bed would be mine.

I walked over to Preston and stood directly in front of him, expecting him to notice me and look up when he reached a stopping point. Preston's eyes remained firmly on his screen, and after a few seconds, I said his name. No acknowledgment. I tried again, louder. "Preston?" Those headphones really put the cancel in noise canceling. I waved my arm, and still, he didn't budge. Was he sleeping with his eyes open?

I stepped to the side around the small table he had swung off the couch arm and touched his shoulder. Preston jumped six inches in the air, scrambling to take his headphones off. "Shit, sorry," he said, his chest heaving as he tried to catch his breath. I put my arms in the air in the international gesture for I mean no harm.

"Sorry, I didn't mean to scare you. I've been trying to get your attention for a minute."

Preston drug his hand through his hair, looking almost embarrassed.

"Ah, yeah, I have this *work zone* I get into where I'm pretty dead to the rest of the world. It's really convenient for working in public places, but often results in jump scares like the one you just gave me. What's up?"

I found myself unable to stop the small smile Preston inspired with his response. This guy was such an earnest nerd. It was endearing. And a little bit cute.

"I just wondered which side of the bed you slept on. I wanted to get some stuff situated on the other side."

"Which side of the bed . . . you mean, we're going to share?"

"I'm sure as hell not going to sleep on this abomination you call a couch. I have no idea how you're sitting there that long to work."

Preston reddened. "It *is* an old couch. I'm never in danger of falling asleep while I work when I sit here. But I'm sure I can figure out how to make it workable to sleep on. You can have the bed."

I almost felt bad, but there was no way in hell I'd survive on that couch for more than a night or two. Lack of sleep alone was terrible for my stomach, but it also made me crave bad foods that were certain to trigger my IBS.

"It's your apartment. You're definitely not sleeping on the couch. We're two adults. We can't share?"

He looked at me like I suggested he never vote again, not simply proposing two adults share a single bed.

"Correct. We're two adults who are practically strangers. And you want to share a bed?" He said this slowly, like if he took long enough, his message would sink in.

I rolled my eyes.

"We'll build a pillow wall, or maybe you have a board for bundling, if you're that worried about your virtue. But that reminds me, we need to work on making touching each other look natural before tonight. Do you need to finish anything up before we start getting ready?"

Preston glanced between his laptop screen and my face.

"And here I thought you just meant showering and getting dressed."

"I mean, we can do that together too, if you want . . ." I got the exact shade of pink out of Preston's cheeks as I hoped I would. Teasing him was far too easy.

"I didn't mean, I thought just, not showering . . ." He stumbled over his words, his brain seeming to short-circuit.

I put him out of his misery. "I just meant simple touches. Hand holding, leading me by my back, not jumping when I put my hand on your shoulder, dancing. You know, the basics."

"I only jumped because I didn't hear or see you. I'm not *that* bad at this."

"Okay, then, prove it."

Preston stared at me, seeming to steel himself. He stood up and walked over to me.

"Let's start with dancing," he said, pulling out his phone and selecting a song. A soft, crooning voice rose from the small speaker.

"Go big or go home. I like it," I said, waiting for him to set the phone down and walk the rest of the way to me. I put one hand on his shoulder and the other tucked into the dip in his waist above his hip. He matched my position, using the large hand that covered most of my small back to pull me incrementally closer. We started to spin in place in time to the song.

"So, have you done a lot of fake relationships in your life? You seem to have quite the list of touches prepared."

I shook my head, meeting his eyes.

"No, this is a first for me. I guess you could say I'm into watching people."

I heard it as soon it was out of my mouth. Preston barked out a laugh, and I used the hand on his shoulder to smack him gently in admonishment, a snicker escaping despite my best intentions.

"Not like that, sicko. It's just . . . I observe people and the way they interact with each other. Are their touches natural or strained? Can they not keep their hands to themselves, just counting down the moments until they rip each other's clothes off? Are they keeping up appearances for the people they're with but their motions are cold and filled with unsaid, angry words? You can tell a lot by touching."

"And that's all from your time as a reporter."

I shook my head. "Not entirely, but it wasn't unhelpful when I was chasing a story and trying to uncover the truth." Observing people as a novelist was an occupational hazard, especially when you spent a lot of time in public alone. Making up back stories for people out together ranked among my favorite ways to pass time, and often resulted in something I could use in one of my books

Preston looked like he wanted to push for more from me, but decided against it. He rolled his fingers along my shoulder, readjusting his grip.

"So, how are we touching right now? Like strangers?"

I shook my head again. "Not quite strangers, but right now, our body language points more to a single-digit-date-type couple. Not sure it's quite at engaged level."

Preston searched my face with his eyes, seeming to decide

something before pulling me flush against his body. The hand on my shoulder curled into my hair to rest my head in the space next to his neck. I found myself closing my eyes, breathing him in, as his thumb moved up and down on my back in gentle strokes.

"How's this then?" he asked, my cheek feeling his voice rumbling from his chest.

Just then, the song ended, the silence ringing through the apartment. I pushed myself back, my body flushed.

"That'll definitely do if there's any dancing. And we covered other touches by starting with the dancing. So smart. And efficient. I'm . . . I'm going to go take a shower now, start the rest of the getting ready process." *Now whose brain was short-circuiting, Jax?*

Preston nodded, his face hard to read.

"There's an extra towel for you hanging in the bathroom. It's the blue one, mine's red."

"Thank you," I said before I raced into the only separate room in the place. I closed the door behind me and leaned against it, needing to put something solid between me and Preston Brandt. My mind raced over the last fifteen minutes, trying to square the Preston who got so easily embarrassed at my low-level flirting with the Preston who faced a challenge head on and held me like it came naturally to him.

"It's not real, it's not real." I repeated to myself as I moved to get undressed and turn on the water in the shower. His willingness to engage, the way those blue eyes pierced mine, the way he seemed to want to know more than my practiced and reserved responses. The result was disarming, especially for a girl who had been on her own for as long as me. I may have just met my match.

CHAPTER

Six

PRESTON

It had been years since I shared a living space with anyone. Growing up, I'd shared a room with my brother Spencer for a while, but sharing a mostly square space with your youngest brother was nothing like sharing it with your *fake fiancée.* My thoughts stuttered a bit as I turned over those words in my mind. What in the world was I going to tell my family? I hated the idea of lying to them, but it seemed like it flew in the face of the benefits of a fake relationship when too many people knew the truth. Laurel already knew it wasn't real. How many people in the know created a liability?

My hands cradled my head as the water from the shower shut off, unsure how I found myself here. I had never thought about any decision less in my life before I made it, and never thought about any decision more in the time since. There were just so many ways it could backfire and blow up in our faces.

I knew I needed to get it together before Jax came back out here. She presented herself so collected and aloof. I didn't want to let her know our situation—living and otherwise—got to me. During our dancing practice, I managed to hold my own. I just need to channel that energy. Fake it till you make it and all that.

With a nod to seal the deal—with myself—I stood up and headed over to the kitchen to wash the three dishes I used so far today, just for something to do.

The bathroom door opened out of sight, but even if the sound hadn't alerted me, the steamy air carrying the scent of jasmine and lavender would have. I took a deep breath in, inhaling the pleasant scent. Eventually, Jax entered my line of sight. The blue towel I set out for her wrapped tightly around her body in that magical way all women seemed to know by the time they were showering around men. Did towel manufacturers offer a secret course on how to drive men you just moved in with wild? How did they keep it a secret?

She bent over to rummage in her drawer of the dresser, causing the towel to ride low and high at the same time. That towel seemed a lot wider when I folded it out of the dryer than it did spanning Jax's torso. I turned my gaze back to the glass drying in my hand, plunging it back under the water in an instant, the hot water a shock to my system. I hope she didn't catch me looking at her in her towel. My eyes locked on the mug rack in front of me, laser focused so they didn't stray. Anything to keep my attention off my very attractive, mostly naked roommate.

"So how long until we need to leave for this thing?" Jax asked, her voice calm and steady, seemingly unaware of my racing thoughts.

I answered, still not looking at her. "We need to be there by 5:30, so I've scheduled a car to pick us up at five." My voice held steady. *Keep it up, Brandt.*

"Okay, great. Do you want to jump in the shower now, and I'll finish up after you're done?"

Turning to answer, I found her applying lotion to her long legs, her wet hair dangling from where her head was turned upside down to reach her ankles. A strangled noise climbed up my throat, desperate to escape. I covered my mouth with my fist, attempting to turn it into a cough.

"Um, yeah sure. I'll head in there now." I moved to the dresser to grab a pair of boxers. After another moment, I grabbed a shirt and pair of shorts; as many layers as possible couldn't hurt this scenario. The lavender of Jax's lotion reached my nose again.

"That lotion smells great. The scent is nice and light. So many lotions can be so fragrant heavy," I found myself saying. *What the hell? Why am I talking about fragrances?*

Jax flipped her hair over her shoulder, lifting her head to meet my eyes with a smile. "I totally agree. This is the only lotion I buy. Plus, it makes your skin extra soft. You're welcome to use it if you want."

The mixture of thinking of Jax's soft skin, and the silky feel of *her* lotion while I jerked my cock up and down entered my mind unbidden. I ground out a "thanks" and cleared the distance to the bathroom in what seemed like three steps. I closed the door behind me and leaned against it, Jax's scent was even more overpowering in the steamy room. My cock plumped the rest of the way up and I squeezed myself once through my pants before releasing just as quickly. My self-control disappeared around this woman. I saw many a cold shower in my future if I didn't get acclimated to having her in my space.

Jax and I managed to orbit each other in the apartment while we finished getting ready. Our movements carried an ease that surprised me for two people who barely knew each other.

"Can you zip me up?" Jax came out of the bathroom, her brown hair falling in loose waves over her shoulders, her forehead covered by artfully messy bangs. She turned her back toward me and I worked the zipper up on her navy dress. I tried to make as little contact with her skin as possible. She turned around to face me, fidgeting with the skirt of the dress. The dress was modest, very appropriate for a Senate campaign dinner. As the Rolodex of guests whirred in my mind, I knew she'd be one of the most beautiful women there.

"You look great," I said, realizing I had been staring.

"Well thank you, fiancé," Jax purred, a wide smile on her face. "You don't clean up half bad yourself."

"I wear a suit literally every day to work. There's nothing exciting about my outfit."

"How do you know I don't wear this every day?" Jax asked while she put earrings in her ears. "Besides, you're adding a shiny new accessory tonight—a fiancée on your arm."

I let out a laugh.

"Yes, I guess you're right. Also, speaking of shiny accessories, I think you're going to need this."

I reached into my pocket and pulled out a ring box. Her eyes homed in on it immediately.

"Is that what I think it is?"

"Well, yeah," I said dumbly. "Last I checked, the engagement ring is a pretty important part of being engaged."

"I figured we'd just say the ring was getting resized or something."

"Oh," I nodded. "I mean, I guess that would have worked for tonight, but eventually . . ."

"Yeah, eventually," Jax said, her eyes still trained on the box in my hand.

"Do you want to see it?"

Jax nodded, her bottom lip between her teeth, the rest of her face unreadable.

I opened the box and handed it to her, box and all.

"Wow, it's beautiful," Jax said, removing the ring from its velvet covered perch.

"My mom died when I was ten. My dad remarried a wonderful woman after I started college. She found out my dad still had a bunch of Mom's old jewelry and asked the youngest four of us if we'd like rings made of one of the pieces for us when and if we needed it. I had her make one for me a years ago when . . . well, in any case, I have this ring now."

Jax stared at me, her expression hard to read. I thought I saw a flicker of understanding pass through before her eyes returned to the ring in her hand. As the silence stretched on, my tie suddenly felt tighter around my neck, my sleeves constricting my arms.

"You don't have to wear it. We can get something else. It's dumb," I said, my face heating. I reached to take it back from her.

Jax moved the ring out of my reach, sliding it onto the fourth finger of her left hand. "No way. It's perfect. Thank you for letting me wear it." She held her hand out, admiring the way the diamond sparkled in the artificial lighting of my living room. The main stone sat between two small pieces of sapphire, my mom's birthstone, on a band of white gold.

We stood in silence for a few beats.

"That was a weird moment, right?" Jax said, breaking the silence, and once again, saying exactly what she had on her mind.

"Somehow, not the weirdest moment I've had today, and probably not the weirdest we'll have tonight." Jax looked inquisitive, like she wanted to know more, but the vibration on my watch forced me to drag my eyes away from hers.

"Our car's almost here. Shall we?" I busied myself with grabbing my wallet and keys. She slipped on her grey wool coat, and I followed her out the door, locking the apartment behind us.

We slid into the backseat of the car, which pulled away from the curb, taking us toward the dinner venue at a hotel in the Northwest part of the city.

The driver listened to NPR, playing a review of a new memoir written by a former child star. This made me think of Charlotte and whether she would have read it yet, which reminded me she and Hayden would be there tonight. I couldn't believe I hadn't thought of that earlier. Fuck. How could I have forgotten? Too much brain space allotted to fragrances.

Trying to sound nonchalant, I said, "Oh, I should probably tell you, my brother Hayden and his girlfriend will be at the dinner tonight."

Jax twisted to look at me, her eyes wide in the dusky light of the evening.

"What? Why?"

"Charlotte, that's his girlfriend, works for a non-profit focusing on independent bookstores that the senator is a big champion of, so they've been invited, along with Charlotte's boss. Honestly, Duncan, my older brother, would probably be there too if he wasn't traveling this weekend. His company donates to the senator."

"I'm sorry. Let me expand my question: What do you mean your brother will be there? Why didn't you tell me that hours ago?"

I let my forced calm slip, some of her panic seeping into my tone. "I'm sorry, you're right. There's just been a lot to keep track of and the fact that they'd be there slipped my mind."

"Well, catch hold of that thought. Quick, Brandt. Are we going to"—she darted a quick look in the driver's direction—"tell them the truth? Or go with the flow?"

"I don't know," I said honestly.

"Well, it's your family, so it's your call. You've mentioned three brothers so far, two of which seem to live here in DC. From the photos, there's one more who hasn't come up. That's potentially problematic, at least four more people knowing, but I won't make you lie to them."

I nodded. "Hayden and Duncan are the only ones here full time. Spencer is finishing up his post-doc and Hunter still lives in Holly Ridge near my dad and Margaret. They both visit a decent amount, though."

Jax nodded. I could almost see her locking the information away for later.

"What do you want to do in regard to telling your family?" I asked, wanting to be sure we were on the same page.

"That won't be a problem," Jax responded, her face suddenly devoid of all emotion.

The car moved on while we sat in silence for a few moments. The roll of the tires on the pavement and the honking horns from drivers frustrated by the Friday night rush hour traffic joined the quiet chatter of the radio. Staring at the passing blocks, I came to a decision.

"I won't tell them. They'll have some questions, but it won't entirely surprise them. It wouldn't be entirely out of character to show up with a serious partner. There's only one area of my life I've ever been known to be impulsive, and this falls under that category."

I saw in her eyes when her analytical mind pieced together exactly why I had a commissioned ring so readily available to give her. Jax nodded, a look of understanding on her face.

My phone dinged in my pocket. A message from Mitchell with a question about his speech that evening awaited me. We rode the rest of the way in silence while I made the changes he requested and reached out to my contact at the hotel. I hoped we'd be able to use a printer on the premises to print an updated version.

The car arrived at the curb of The Dupont Circle Hotel and I got out, walking quickly over to the curb side of the car to open Jax's door and helped her out onto the sidewalk. The hand she placed in mine for balance twisted in my palm and our fingers interlocked. I glanced down quickly at our entangled hands and then up at her face.

"Ready?" she asked, her smile genuine and reassuring all at once.

"Ready or not," I said, smiling back.

We mingled a bit before dinner. I briefly abandoned Jax while I followed a hotel employee to a dark office and made a new copy of the speech for the senator that evening. I returned to find her engaged in conversation with one of our largest donors, her laugh carrying to my ears twenty feet away. I smiled and walked up to the group, sliding my hand onto her lower back, just like we had practiced.

"So this sparkling young woman is here with you this evening, Preston?" Donovan Fitzgerald asked, reaching out to shake my hand in greeting.

"Yes, she sure is. This is my fiancée, Jacqueline." I introduced her the way she had in my office yesterday. She smiled up at me, pleased I had picked up on the subtle detail of how she preferred to be addressed in professional settings.

"Oh, I love meet cutes," Donovan's wife, Olivia, practically squealed. "Please tell me how you all met."

I looked down at Jax, unsure how we hadn't anticipated this question. My gut started to knot in panic. "Well," I opened my mouth to start spewing bullshit, when I felt Jax's hand on my arm.

"It's my turn to tell the story, sweetie," she said, and I snapped my jaw shut, happy to have her take the lead on this one.

"I was a reporter, covering politics in the city. We kept crossing paths at different events, Preston always made eyes at me from across the room. Finally, I walked up to him and said, 'Will you just ask me out already?' He did, and well, here we are."

The group laughed at my expense and I found myself joining in because it fit like a story plucked from my actual life.

At that moment, a member of the hotel staff came up to our group and encouraged us to find our seats. Hands were shaken, promises of lunches and drinks exchanged, and Jax and I headed for table three.

"I made eyes at you, huh?"

Jax smiled up at me, as I pulled out her chair.

"Your eyes tell the story, Preston."

After everyone took their seats for dinner, I scoured the room for Hayden. I didn't find him at any of the tables. Noticing movement by the doors, I spotted him and Charlotte sneaking in late to join the party. From Charlotte's flushed cheeks and my brother's shit-eating grin, it wasn't hard to guess what had delayed them.

Our eyes met, and I rolled my eyes at him, softening it with a smile. He waved his hand in greeting at the same moment Jax laid her hand on my arm. I leaned in to hear her, laughing gently at her joke. My gaze returned to Hayden's. He glanced quizzically between Jax and myself, nudging Charlotte and pointing—somewhat obviously—to the two of us. She pulled his hand down, shaking her head at his behavior, leading him toward the empty seats at their table. The look Hayden speared me with before he turned to help Charlotte into her seat left no room for doubt. I'd be getting the third degree from my younger brother before the night was out.

CHAPTER
Seven

JAX

I've never attended a political fundraising dinner before, but it didn't surprise me to find few differences than standing on a press line. Well, less shouting and more drinking than most press lines, but still. The schmoozing skills I picked up over the years working for different news outlets transferred directly. Preston found himself pulled away from the table several times to talk to this person or that, once by the senator to go over something else in the speech.

"Oh, he's not finished," I said, stopping the waiter from taking away Preston's plate. His food had probably grown cold by now, but I wanted to be sure he had a chance to eat more.

"Sorry about that," Preston said, sitting back down at the table. "Oh, my food's still here?" He looked surprised.

"Oh yeah . . . I wasn't sure if you were done or not, so I asked them not to take it when they came back around the last time." I started to fidget with my napkin, worried I committed some sort of faux pas.

A wide grin split Preston's face. "Thank you. I never get to eat at these things. They always take my plate because no one's here to stop them."

I returned his smile, the knots in my stomach untwisting.

"Fiancée perks," I said, raising my glass in a toast.

"Fiancée perks," he responded, clinking his glass with mine.

The rest of the seated portion of the dinner went smoothly. While the senator gave his speech, everyone's eyes were glued on him, but I couldn't stop watching Preston. He mouthed the words along with his boss at certain parts. I could picture him up on the stage, being the center of it all. A shame I wouldn't be around to see it.

Applause broke me out of my reverie, and I saw the senator walking away from the lectern on the stage, shaking hands with those seated at the tables closest to him.

"So now what?" I asked Preston, leaning close to murmur in his ear.

"Now, we shake more hands, drink more drinks, and try to avoid the dance floor."

"Not a big dancer, Brandt? Things went okay this afternoon." Preston's cheeks turned pink.

"I can manage turning in a slow circle, you're right. It's more out of habit than anything."

I leaned on his shoulder with my elbow, bringing my face next to his. I had no real reason to be this close to him. Simply sitting together and talking was pulling off the facade just fine, but it felt right.

"Well, I think your fiancée might like it if you spun in slow circles outside of your living room."

"Well then, we might just need to make that happen," Preston responded, his eyes locked on mine. From this close, I could see the speckles of caramel and gold in his eyes.

A throat cleared behind us, causing us to jump apart.

I turned around to see a blond woman and a man who bore more than a passing resemblance to Preston standing there.

"Well, hi there, big brother. How great to see you here. Anyone you want to introduce us to?" his brother asked, the look on his face accusatory.

Preston sighed the heavy sigh of a put-upon older brother, standing up to shake hands and give the woman a hug.

"Hayden, Charlotte, I'd like to introduce you to Jax."

I stood, offering my hand out to shake. "It's really nice to meet you both." Hayden took my extended hand, shaking it, but looked distracted. He continued to eye Preston, expecting more explanation. Charlotte rolled her eyes and took my hand after Hayden dropped it.

"You'll have to excuse Hayden. Sometimes he's incapable of keeping up basic social norms."

"Well, you would be too if you saw your workaholic brother with a date in public for the first time in years. I don't think I've heard of you with anyone at an event like this since—"

"Hayden, Charlotte, it's good to see you. Thanks for joining us tonight." A new voice joined the conversation.

Preston seemed saved from the trip down memory lane by the appearance of the senator, having finally made his way through the crowd to where we sat.

Hayden managed to shake the senator's hand with more grace than he had mine. "That was a great speech, sir. It's great to hear about your plans for education and literacy in your next term. You know that's a cause important to us." Hayden slipped his arm around Charlotte's waist, who in turn placed her hand on Hayden's chest. They moved with the familiarity of two people who had found their match. Preston and I should take notes.

"Well, thank you. I can only take credit for the delivery. You know how lucky I am to have your brother putting words into the best order possible for me." The senator turned his eyes to Preston and me.

"Jax, it's great to see you. I'm so glad you convinced your fiancé to bring you out of hiding and join us this evening."

I felt Preston wince as Hayden choked on the sip of whiskey he took before the senator started talking.

"Yes, I'm glad things are all out in the open. Can you excuse us for a minute, sir? I'll catch up with you later to debrief?"

The senator nodded, unaware of the grenade he just tossed, his eyes already searching for the next person to glad-hand.

"I'm sorry, *what?*" Hayden started his questioning a bit louder than socially acceptable.

"Not here," Preston gritted out, smiling at everyone who looked over at us, grabbing Hayden's arm and steering him to the back of the room.

I fell in step with Charlotte as we followed them through the space.

"So, Preston mentioned you worked for a non-profit?"

Charlotte smiled at me as we dodged other guests. "Yes, I work for the Independent Bookstore Alliance as a Development Associate. We have resources that help keep independent bookstores afloat when they run into troubled times." As a reader and an author, there was nothing I loved more than a good bookstore, especially an independent one with booksellers championing their favorite novels. I had a good feeling Charlotte and I would get along, while I was around at least.

"Oh, that's great. I love a good bookstore, especially one with a good romance section," I said, practiced in hiding my writing identity under the guise of a bibliophile.

"A girl after my own heart. We'll have to talk more about that when we have more time and my boyfriend's head isn't close to exploding," Charlotte said as we exited the ballroom and turned left.

I let out a surprised laugh. "You seem to handle the unexpected well."

"I haven't been around the Brandt brothers all that long, but one thing I know for sure is they're full of surprises."

"I'll have to keep that in mind."

"Besides, right now, I'm the only non-Brandt at family dinners other than their stepmom, Margaret. As long as you love each other, I'm not too pressed about how this all came to be. I'll just be glad to have someone to share incredulous looks with."

Keeping the same smile on my face suddenly took more effort. Not having any living immediate family meant you didn't have to deal with familial expectations. It surprised me to find myself susceptible to the ones Charlotte was leveraging at me, all in good faith, since she thought Preston and I were really engaged.

Preston and Hayden came to a dead stop at the end of a corridor around the corner from the ballroom.

"Springing a fucking fiancée on us, Preston? Are you kidding me?"

"Hey now," Preston said. "Watch yourself."

Hayden took a deep breath, his eyes turning to me.

"I'm sorry, Jax. I didn't mean any offense. I'm sure you're wonderful if my brother loves you. I'm just extremely caught off guard."

I put my hands up in a conciliatory gesture. "No offense taken here. I understand it being a surprise."

"How long have you been dating? Have you been lying to us when we asked you if you were seeing anyone? Pardon the phrasing, but seriously, bro, what the fuck?"

"We've been in each other's orbits for a while now with her former job as a reporter and my job with the senator. We finally went out for the first time a few months ago, and I didn't say anything because I wasn't sure where things were going. I didn't want to introduce her to the whole Brandt circus unnecessarily. Then suddenly, earlier this week, things weren't so casual anymore, and now here we are."

Hayden took a step closer to Preston and lowered his voice, trying to make sure Charlotte and I couldn't hear, but he wasn't nearly far enough away.

"But, are you sure? I mean, this isn't like—"

"Enough," Preston said, his tone so forceful Hayden stepped back. "I understand where you're coming from, but I'm going to need you to trust me when I say that what Jax and I have is nothing like any relationship I've had before. I'd appreciate it if you could keep this news to yourself for a little while, so I can be the one to let everyone else know."

Hayden nodded, struck silent. Charlotte's eyes were wide, darting back and forth between all of us, but she kept quiet as well.

"Now, if you'll excuse us, I promised my fiancée a dance at our first public event together. Maybe we can all get dinner sometime soon?"

Silence hung in the air for a beat more before Charlotte ended it. "We'd love that. Just name the time and place. We'll be there."

Preston nodded, putting a hand on his brother's shoulder briefly before holding that same arm out to me and escorting me back to the ballroom. Preston's eyes stayed resolutely on the hallway in front of us, but I snuck a peek over my shoulder, where Hayden watched us leave as Charlotte wrapped her arm around his back.

Preston stayed silent as we reentered the ballroom, working our way toward the dance floor. We stopped in the middle of the crowd, blending in with the rest of the couples moving to the slow melody coming from the speakers. Preston put his arm on my shoulder and took my hand in his, duplicating our dance posture from earlier today.

We swayed in a slow circle for a bit before I found myself unable to take the silence any longer.

"So, that went well . . ."

Preston bent his head so it was resting on my shoulder, and I felt his shoulders start to shake.

"Hey, it's okay. It seemed like he started to come around to things . . ."

I trailed off as Preston brought his head back up, and I saw laughter on his face, not tears.

"I can't believe the senator outed us like that, so casually. I think maybe he thought we were lying and wanted to see if calling us out in front of my brother would call my bluff. What a mess."

His shoulders stopped moving, and he let out a huge sigh.

"Well, now Hayden knows, so hopefully the senator's doubts are assuaged. Will Hayden really not tell the rest of your family? Or can we expect more confused phone calls? Assuming you still want to tell them? That did seem a little rough."

Preston's hand started to draw small circles on my back.

"I didn't like lying to him. But he'll give me a few days to tell them, even if it kills him to do so. My brothers are terrible gossips. And I've ripped the Band-Aid off now. One brother down, three to go. As long as you're still okay with this. I don't want you to feel like collateral damage to my family's dynamics."

I shook my head.

"I'm good if you're good."

Preston nodded and his eyes roved around the room as we continued to spin in place on the dance floor.

"You know what would really convince the senator if he did still have doubts," I said slowly.

Preston's eyes returned to mine. "What's that?"

"A public display of affection."

Preston's eyes widened. I should stop this train of thought, even though I'm the one who launched it from the station. That interaction with his brother mixed things up inside me enough.

"More than slow dancing in a crowded room, you mean?"

I nodded, not able to stop my gaze straying to his lips.

"Oh," Preston said, his shoulders rising with a big breath in. "You're not wrong. A kiss would certainly help with the legitimacy of our relationship."

"I'm up for it if you are." At this point, I wanted to feel his lips on mine more than I wanted to protect my boundaries. Seeing him grapple with hurting Hayden made me want to reassure him, to comfort him. Apparently, through his mouth.

Preston laughed. "What every guy wants to hear."

Nonetheless, Preston's face moved incrementally closer to mine, my eyes fluttering closed, waiting and anticipating . . .

"Sorry to interrupt, but Preston, I need to speak with you."

Preston and I jerked apart.

"N-Now?" Preston stuttered.

"Yes, now," the senator said, his tone indicating his displeasure with Preston's question, but at least he realized he couldn't go full asshole mode with so many people around. "Raymond Olson is here and just had a cancellation for tomorrow morning on *Political Pulse*. We need to shorten tonight's speech to fit the talking head format."

"Got it," Preston said. "I'll be right with you. I want to get Jax situated to get home first."

The senator's mouth formed a thin line as he looked over at me, seeming displeased he no longer had immediate and unfettered access to my fiancé. "Fine, I'll see you in five minutes."

Without a parting word, the senator turned and walked away, directing his attention toward a group gathered on the side of the dance floor.

"I'm not sure your boss likes me too much . . ." I said, fidgeting, not meeting Preston's eyes after our almost kiss.

"Nah. Well, that might be true, but honestly, he doesn't like anyone, so try not to take it personally."

I laughed. "Good, I'd be worried about securing a job with him otherwise."

Preston pushed his glasses back up on his nose. "I'll take care of it. I'll lay the groundwork tonight as we're talking. That we're having to work tonight for a TV spot opens the door for needing a Comms Director person nicely. Now, let's get you a car home."

"I can handle it," I said, pulling my phone out of my purse and starting to call up a ride share app.

Preston's hand landed on my arm. "I know you can, but what kind of fiancé would I be if I just let you wait outside on your own?"

"You don't have time for that."

Preston put light pressure on my lower back to get me moving. "Maybe I'll make the senator wait for me for just a bit longer. Might give him a complex. Could be fun."

I laughed. The more I learned about Preston's personality, the more the layers I discovered surprised me. He was more than an uptight, perfectionist I discounted him for when we met. Learning more felt dangerous.

We walked to the front of the hotel and waited in comfortable silence, me watching the car's progress on my app, Preston looking around, taking in the bustle around us.

Finally, my car pulled into the drive.

"Well, this is me. I guess I'll see you later tonight?"

Preston nodded, looking conflicted at sending me back by myself.

"I'll be fine. I've been putting myself to bed for years now," I teased.

Preston smiled. "I suppose that's true. Don't feel like you need to wait up. I have no idea how long this'll be."

It all felt so domestic, like Preston and I had parted ways knowing we'd return to the same place many nights before. I reached up on tiptoes to press a chaste kiss on his cheek.

"Bye, fiancé," I said, sliding into the car and shutting the door behind me.

Preston lifted his hand in a wave as the car started to move, a stunned look still on his face.

BRANDT BROTHERS GROUP CHAT

PRESTON

All right, I have some news.

HUNTER

You won the lottery.

DUNCAN

The Euro crashed.

SPENCER

The senator finally asked for my number.

HAYDEN

Some might say Preston's secured himself a prize...

PRESTON

And it's because of Hayden and his lack of restraint I'm sharing this news via text at midnight, please remember that.

Also, Spencer, no. Never.

DUNCAN

Out with it already, it's 6 a.m. here. Time is money.

                                        PRESTON

                              Well, I'm engaged.

SPENCER

To be MARRIED?

HUNTER

The fuck?

DUNCAN

Are you sure you've thought this through? I didn't even know you were dating anyone.

HAYDEN

My reactions exactly.

HUNTER

Oh shut up, Hay. We know you're secretly thrilled you found out first.

                                        PRESTON

                    Her name is Jax. She's going to be working for
                    the senator with me.

HUNTER

Again, I say, the fuck?

                                        PRESTON

                         I'm really feeling the love guys.

DUNCAN

If you're happy, we're happy, Preston. It's just…

PRESTON

Well, gotta go. The senator needs my full attention.

SPENCER

Honestly, I think I'd be less surprised if he said he was engaged to Marsden.

HUNTER

So, while he's busy, spill the details, Hayden. What's she like? Is she like you-know-who?

HAYDEN

I'll give exclusive details to whomever offers me the best bribe in a private message.

Make that tomorrow morning. Charlotte's drawing us a bath.

HUNTER

My eyessssss.

DUNCAN

You're all going to turn me grey.

SPENCER

Hate to break it to you...

HUNTER

You're already there.

CHAPTER
Eight

PRESTON

My phone read after 1:00 a.m. when I finally unlocked the door to my—and now Jax's—apartment. I winced at the squeaking sound as I pushed it slowly open. I took a step into the apartment, the floor creaking slightly under my weight, and narrowly avoided ramming into an end table in the dark room. *Who knew this place was such a noisy deathtrap*, I thought, waking up the screen of my phone to cast a slight glow on the room.

I walked into the bathroom, finally turning on a light. The reflection in the mirror showed a tired man in his thirties, with his tie loosened and his overcoat still on against the cold. I started stripping off layers, piling them in the corner of the bathroom where they'd sit until I could safely deal with them in the main room.

After splashing water on my face and brushing my teeth, I turned the lights back off and opened the door. Blinking, I let my eyes adjust to the darkness again, realizing too late that I was about to creep across the apartment in only my boxer briefs. *I think I have some pajama bottoms in that middle drawer*, I thought, carefully working my way to the dresser.

I slid the drawer out silently and started rifling through the carefully folded clothes, packed a bit tighter than normal now that I had made room for Jax's clothing. I was just complimenting myself on my ninja skills when a bright light from the direction of the bed made me freeze in my tracks.

"What the actual fuck are you doing? Building a fortress?" I couldn't make Jax out behind the spotlight coming from her phone.

"I'm looking—"

"Oh shit. Put some clothes on." The light fell to the bedcovers.

"That's what I'm trying to do." I picked up my own phone from on top of the dresser and turned a light on, spotting the blue and green plaid pattern of the pants in question.

"I mean, in other circumstances, I'd totally take a bite out of that ass. Just so you're aware that my outburst did not come from a place of repulsion."

Jax's voice was muffled, and I looked over to see her arm flung across her face. I couldn't help but smile.

"Good to know," I said, pulling the pants on and approaching the bed. "I'm sorry for the free show. I thought you were asleep, and, well, old habits die hard. There hasn't been anyone to peep on me going to bed for a long time."

"I wasn't peeping," Jax exclaimed, sounding indignant. "You woke me up."

"And what an enjoyable experience middle-of-the-night Jax has been," I said, sliding into my side of the bed and running my hip into a pillow Jax had placed there as a barrier.

"What time is it anyway?" Jax asked, the sound of her phone being set on the bookshelf next to her side of the bed mixing with the rustling covers as she got comfortable.

"One forty-five," I said, unlocking my phone and flipping quickly through the notifications, making sure nothing needed my attention before I went to sleep.

"God, I can't wait to work for this man too."

"Honestly, once you start, it'll be better for both of us. Mitchell agreed to meet with you on Monday, by the way. He said he'll do the interview, since it would be a conflict of interest for me to hire my fiancée."

"Well, at least there's that. Now, please, shut up," Jax said through a yawn.

"Yes, ma'am," I said, fighting to keep a smile out of my voice, trying not to betray how adorable I found grumpy Jax to be.

I opened the last app I used every night, putting my phone on the charging dock and settling into a comfortable position, my back to Jax.

"Preston?"

"Hmm?"

"What the fuck is that noise?"

"Oh, that's my brown noise app. I can't sleep in silence. Is that okay?"

"What would happen if I said no?"

"Well, I'd turn it off and do my best to sleep."

Jax sighed and said nothing. I interpreted that as her giving in.

"Goodnight, Jax."

"Goodnight."

The last thing I heard before I drifted off to sleep, the exhaustion of my body and the familiar sounds of my noise machine app pulling me under quickly, was Jax saying, "I'm never going to sleep with this."

Several hours later, with light streaming in through the curtains and a warm body plastered to mine, showed just how mistaken she had been.

As my mind came online, I took in how Jax's body aligned with mine. Her shoulders were flush with my chest, our legs entangled, and her ass pressed against my morning wood.

I angled my hips back first, trying to slide the rest of myself away from the still sleeping woman in my bed. Once again, I failed at keeping Jax asleep.

"Well, I guess that pillow wall didn't do its damn job," Jax murmured, her voice deep and raspy from sleep.

"Yeah, sorry about that. I guess we're both heat seekers."

"Speak for yourself, Brandt. I'm not a cuddler. Besides, you're clearly on my side."

I sat up and looked to my right, seeing she was absolutely correct.

"Well, shit." I rubbed my hands down my face. The last time I shared a bed regularly . . . well, it surprised me my body didn't stray further away out of reflex.

"It's fine," she said. "An unconscious body action, a fluke. These things are bound to happen in shared space like this. No big deal. Now, what's for breakfast?"

Unless fluke had another secret meaning, it didn't apply to our cuddling tendencies. It was not a onetime thing. Jax and I woke up the same way Sunday morning and then again on Monday. That third morning, I managed to extricate myself from the bed without waking her. Likely because it was 5:00 a.m., and I learned over the weekend that my new roommate was not a morning person. I found myself taking yet another freezing cold shower. Something had to give, or I was going to develop frostbite on my dick.

Normally my weekday mornings began with C-SPAN on the television, a few cups of coffee, and sorting emails and tasks to tackle on the day ahead. Adding an extra person in my space meant my routine needed to adjust too. Not something I handled well. I pulled on track pants and a hoodie in a rougher manner than necessary. After checking the temperature outside, I ground my teeth and added a vest and beanie for good measure. I preferred to allow the day to warm up before I experienced it, but new routines called for a few sacrifices.

Deciding to go to the café down the street and grab us some breakfast, I thought perhaps I could still salvage my morning habits and sort through the day ahead. Maybe after work I'd suggest we hammer out a new morning routine that worked for us both.

While sitting in the café, enjoying that first cup of coffee and a cheese and bacon soufflé, the solution to one of our problems struck. Gulping down the dregs of my mug, I unearthed my phone and started searching. After a few minutes of comparing options and reading top reviews, I made a choice and placed my order—miles away from my normal decision-making process, but desperate times called for desperate measures.

I practically skipped back to the apartment, carrying a drink holder with two to-go cups and a bag of chocolate croissants. I kept Jax's coffee black, not sure what additives were safe for her stomach. At second thought, the buttery, flakey pastries may also be a terrible choice. I made a mental note to find out more about her safe foods. That term popped up a lot on the IBS websites I found myself scrolling last night while I listened to Jax's even breathing, as sleep evaded me. I dreaded my body betraying me by pulling Jax close while we were both unconscious. If this arrangement was going to work, we needed to enforce clear boundaries, only engaging in intentional physical touch among them.

I found Jax sitting up in bed, looking at her phone, when I reentered the apartment.

"Honey, I'm home," I said, Jax's eyes meeting mine at my jovial tone.

"I'm not so sure honey really suits me as a pet name, but if that coffee is for me, you can call me anything you want," she said, her arms outstretched.

"It is for you. I left it black. I realize I need to get a better handle on your food sensitivities, so I can buy things that work for you."

I crossed the apartment to hand her the cup, and stood, hovering, not quite sure what to do with myself now that I'd delivered her drink.

Jax waved her hand, dismissing my comment. "Not your problem to worry about. Black is perfect. Coffee, in general, isn't the best thing for me, but some mornings won't kick start without it."

She took a big sip, her eyes closing as she savored the warmth and taste.

"So, what were you up so early for, anyway?"

"Five is usually when I start on work days. Weekends too, sometimes."

"Gross. I like to pretend there isn't even one of those in the morning."

I laughed. "Early bird gets the worm and all that. And anyway, my early morning habits paid off this morning, because I found a solution to one of our problems."

"We have problems?" she asked, swinging her legs off the bed and padding over to the paper bag I set on the edge of the TV stand.

"I bought a new couch."

Jax still rustled through the bag, her back to me.

I continued. "You know, so you can have the bed to yourself. I got something new that hasn't been in my family since Duncan went to college, so I think it should be soft enough to sleep on. Maybe I should have gone to a store to try one out . . . I'm not often this impulsive, but we need a new couch, so I got one . . ."

I trailed off when I realized Jax was frozen, her hand in the bag, her back rigid.

"They're chocolate croissants. Like I said, I need to know more about your food restri—"

"You got a new couch?"

"Well yeah," I said, no longer feeling sure of my decision.

"Why?"

"Well, I thought it might be good to have separate spaces to sleep in. You know, so we don't keep . . . magnetically joining each night."

"I see. I didn't realize it was a big problem for you." Jax's voice was like ice. Shit, had I hurt her feelings? She's the one who put the pillow between us every night. I assumed she wanted boundaries, just like I did.

"I mean, it's not a problem per se, I just don't want you to be—"

"What time did you say my meeting with the senator is today?"

My mind scrambled, trying to keep up with our conversation and understand her reaction to my news.

"It's at eleven."

"Got it. Okay, I'm going to go take a shower. I know this is your place, so I don't have any right to ask, but I'd really appreciate it if you weren't here when I got out."

Yep. Definitely pissed. This felt a lot like a fight Spencer told me about when my dad bought a new outdoor patio set without clearing it with Margaret. Did she want to help pick out the new couch? It would stay in my place after . . . after this was all over.

"Okay . . ." I said slowly, trying to tread carefully. "If that's what you want, I can give you some space."

She nodded, avoiding my eyes. She gathered some clothes out of the drawer and headed toward the bathroom.

"Jax . . ." I said, trailing off, not sure what I meant to say next. I just didn't like the idea of us parting like this, even if I'd see her in a few hours.

She avoided my gaze, even as she turned toward me. "Don't worry. I'll be the doting fiancée when I see you. I just need a hot shower to wake up. I'm not a morning person after all." She met my eyes for the first time since I brought up the couch and smiled. The facial movement didn't reach her eyes.

"Okay, I'll see you at the Senate staff entrance at 10:45? I'll meet you there then?"

She nodded and disappeared into the bathroom with a click of the door locking behind her. She felt entirely out of my reach, physically and emotionally. I started getting dressed for the day on autopilot, using water from the sink to fix my hair. I wanted to honor Jax's request, even when it put me at a disadvantage. I thought getting this couch would be a good thing, but it seems I had a lot more to learn about my fake fiancée than I realized.

CHAPTER
Nine

JAX

I knew my behavior this morning could likely be classified as irrational, but there were times I couldn't stop the overwhelming instinct to curl into myself and run away. Preston's casual and unplanned announcement that he purchased a couch for him to sleep on brought those self-protection instincts out in me. Over the weekend, we worked on comms tasks, watched movies, and spent more time getting comfortable being around each other. And then at night . . . I couldn't bring myself to admit I liked waking up with his warmth near me because we were two professionals, helping each other out, nothing more. But at the same time, I couldn't stop the hurt feelings that emerged from hearing his eagerness to sleep away from me.

It's been three fucking nights. Get a grip, Jacqueline, I thought. I knew it was serious whenever I full named myself in my own head.

After the world's longest shower, I emerged into an empty apartment as requested. Guilt immediately flooded my system. This was the first workday of our new arrangement. What had Preston given up by leaving this morning?

The weekend hadn't allowed us any time to learn each other's typical routines. You know, the things normal couples pick up on during months and years of dating. We hadn't even left the apartment to go grocery shopping. What did Preston eat for breakfast in the morning? Did he pack a lunch or eat out most days?

So many things were uncertain. After years of doing everything I could to avoid the uncertainty of my adolescence, the instability of how Preston and I related to each other tied my stomach in knots. I placed my hand there, almost as if I could feel my guts roiling in revolt through my skin. As usual, the coffee ended up being a poor choice, but it had been so nice for Preston to bring it to me.

I took my time getting ready. I unearthed a meditation app from my phone and emerged from the apartment more centered and levelheaded than I had started the day. Maybe the couch wouldn't be such a bad thing after all. In the light of day, I could see that giving us some space from each other may have its benefits. Four hundred square feet was not a ton of space for two people used to functioning on their own.

The sun warmed the February air to unseasonably mild temperatures, though the flush of Preston's cheeks when he had returned from the café told me the day didn't start this way. The walk from Preston's building went quickly as the blue sky provided hope that spring was around the corner in the nation's capital.

I took a deep breath and straightened my interview suit as I opened the outer door to the senator's offices. It was earlier than Preston and I arranged to meet. I hoped we'd have a chance to clear the air before my interview. The security guard recognized me from my press days, and once he saw my name on the list of approved visitors, he let me go right up. Laurel sat at her desk at the front and greeted me with a large smile.

"Jax! It's *so* good to see you. Do you have lunch plans after this? We should really get lunch." Her blue eyes sparkled with humor and insider knowledge. I couldn't help myself from smiling back at her and answering with a slight laugh in my voice. "Um, I'm not sure what my plans for lunch are."

"I'm hoping you'll have lunch with your fiancé to celebrate, and maybe, if she's nice, the annoying interloper can join us," Preston said, appearing from the hallway. Laurel scoffed at being called an interloper, but otherwise didn't press. Her eyes darted back and forth between Preston and me. The tension between us was thick with the awkward way we had left—okay, I made him leave—things this morning.

"I think we shouldn't get too far ahead of ourselves, but if things go well, a celebratory lunch sounds nice," I said, flashing Preston a genuine smile. I watched his shoulders release a few inches, relieved he picked up on the apology laced in my response. I didn't dare be more opaque out in the open.

"Ms. Carter," Senator Marsden greeted us, appearing from the same hallway Preston had moments before. "It'll be so nice to chat with you in a professional capacity. Are you ready now?"

I took his extended hand in a firm shake, not wincing when he squeezed tighter than was politely acceptable. Fine, let's do it this way, cis white man. The one part of being a reporter I enjoyed was eating the egos of men like him for breakfast. I could certainly handle coddling one for a few months, especially for a paycheck.

"I'm looking forward to it, Senator Marsden." I smiled at Laurel and Preston as I followed the senator into his office. He shut the door behind me and gestured to the chair facing his desk. Unsurprisingly, he sat on the other side of the huge wooden monstrosity. Some might think the senator was compensating for something, but I thought it more likely his self-assuredness emanated in part from Big Dick Energy.

"So, Jacqueline, tell me"—the senator put my resume down on his desk after a few moments of silence—"are you applying for this job undercover in your capacity as a reporter, looking to make a fool out of me and my Chief of Staff?"

I had to appreciate his straight shooting. His eyes narrowed as a grin crossed my face, but I couldn't help it. The man understood the political game better than some of his colleagues who had been in office for multiple decades.

"No, sir, that would be incredibly unethical." He opened his mouth to say more, but I kept going. "Not that unethical behavior is out of the ordinary here on the Hill. But that's not my game." Senator Marsden looked slightly impressed I hadn't cowered at his interruption.

"I may not play nice, but ethics are incredibly important to me. Brandt out there doesn't have an unethical bone in his body, and I'm not sure he could sense one in someone else, especially if his dick is involved." The senator leveled me with a cool, steely look that raised my hackles.

"Preston is a great man, and his ethics will make him a great politician one day. You're lucky to have him. I know you know that, and honestly, you should start acting like it once in a while."

He raised one eyebrow at me. "You're a loyal one, aren't you?"

I held tight to the arms of my chair to stop myself from crossing my arms and going completely on the defensive. "I suppose I am."

Senator Marsden leaned forward on the desk, folding his arms and leaning his weight on them. "Ethics and loyalty are the most important aspects I look for in an employee. I know you can do this job—I've read your stuff. You're a good writer, you get to the heart of the issue, and you're not afraid to go for the jugular. It's a style similar to my own." He appraised me for a moment longer. "And you're right. I do know how lucky I am to have Brandt working for me. That's the reason you're here. I don't want to wring him out before he ever gets to launch his own run. He'll be good for his people. I'm an asshole, but not a monster."

I nodded. "Your record speaks for itself. I wouldn't consider working for you if you didn't get things done that I care about."

The senator sat back in his chair, tilting toward the back

wall. "Anything else I need to know before we make this thing official?"

This certainly made a case for the most hostile, but most casual, interview I'd ever experienced. My mind flashed to Mark's email, letting me know I had been let go. I didn't want to tell this man any of my secrets, but I also couldn't blindside him, and thereby Preston, if Peggy Rappencourt came calling again.

"I have another job. It's freelance. I'm my own boss and operate under a different name. It shouldn't interfere with my work here. The nature of that work is empowering to women and, at times explicit, which could raise the hackles of some of your political opponents."

"Are you on OnlyFans?"

My mind replayed what I said, and I barked out a laugh, recognizing how he got there.

"Your time is your business," the senator said, throwing his hands up in the air. "As long as it's safe, legal, and consensual, I don't care how people make their money. I'm just not big on surprises."

"I'm not on OnlyFans, but respect the hell out of people who are," I responded. "I'm a romance author," I said, raising my own eyebrow back at him, waiting for the usual scoff that often accompanied the genre.

To my surprise, he only nodded. "That explains this whirl-wind engagement shit you and Brandt have going on. I don't have space in my life for that fluff, but if you believe in love and can make a living on it, good for you."

Senator Marsden and I were more alike than I would ever admit out loud. Of course, I believed in love, but for others, not for me. I had been alone too long and lost too many important people to risk opening my heart again.

"Well, Laurel will get you the paperwork, and I'll get Brandt to send you all the reading you'll need. Get caught up today and be ready to work tomorrow." The senator stood up, breaking me out of my thoughts, buttoned his suit jacket, and opened the door. He stood beside it, clearly ready to move on with his day.

"Thank you, sir," I said as I exited, and he nodded, his eyes meeting mine. In the brief moment, I knew he recognized parts of himself in me as well.

"And Ms. Carter, make sure you leave any drama with Brandt at home. There's no place for it here."

I rolled my eyes as I walked away, somewhat relieved to have the asshole back in full force and we could move on with the status quo.

I knocked on the wall of Preston's cubicle, unable to stop the smile that spread on my face when he looked up and just looked happy to see me.

"So?" he asked, standing from his desk.

"I guess we need to agree on a place to go for lunch," I answered, smiling back.

"I never had any doubts." Preston enveloped me in a hug. While his arms wrapped around me, something twinged in my gut at how much I liked telling someone my good news. A good, but dangerous, feeling.

"Well, I never thought we'd need an office PDA policy because of you, Preston. Strange things happen every day." Laurel appeared behind us, her tone teasing.

"And because of that, you're definitely not invited to lunch," Preston said, releasing me, but kept his hand on my back. It already seemed like second nature to him to be touching me. The twinging intensified.

"Lunch?" Senator Marsden came out to join our little group. "Not today, Brandt. I need you with me at the weekly committee briefing. Hopefully, they'll have tuna salad, your favorite." As quickly as he appeared, he left again, exiting the office suite.

"I hate tuna salad," Preston grumbled. I made a mental note, trying not to smile at his annoyed face.

"I can still grab lunch with you if you want?" Laurel leaned against the doorjamb, her smile genuine and inviting.

"Thanks, but I think I need to get home and get reading, so I'm ready to start tomorrow. Plus, we have that couch delivery happening this afternoon. Right, sweetie?" Preston tensed beside me. Was it the sweetie or the couch that got that reaction? "But definitely lunch, or maybe even drinks after work, another time soon," I said, directing my gaze at Laurel.

"Drinks, yes, absolutely. We'll go to Union Pub, get you all anointed into the Senate staffer culture. I'll go get your paperwork together so you can take that home too." With that, Laurel flounced back to her desk.

"Are you sure you're okay waiting for the couch delivery?" Preston asked once Laurel was out of earshot. "I know you were questioning the . . . color we went with." His eyes searched mine.

"I think you were right about the color," I said firmly, but gently. "It'll go really well in the space."

Preston nodded, his face suddenly unreadable. "I paid extra to have them take the old couch out too, so it should be pretty simple, but call me if you need anything. I'll email you all the documents you'll need for your afternoon reading assignment."

"That'll be great. I'll see you tonight." I turned to walk to Laurel's desk, pausing at the doorway. "Maybe we can go grocery shopping tonight? Or at least do a grocery delivery order?" Even though I knew we needed the space the couch would provide, I still wanted to know things about this man. What type of yogurt did he eat? Did he have a preferred type of bread or a favorite pasta shape? Did he even ever eat at home?

"That sounds great, Jax. I'll see you at home."

CHAPTER
Ten

PRESTON

Given we lived in a shared space with very few walls, I found myself bumping into Jax's boundaries the rest of the week. I felt forgiven for whatever slight she interpreted from my couch buying, but a distance existed that hadn't been there before. Which was ridiculous when I thought about it, because of course there would be distance. We were two people who barely knew each other.

We went to work, where I got to see Jacqueline. She had sharp instincts, her voice for press releases and other materials was perfect, and she seemed to have no fear when chasing down an opportunity or appearance. At home, that facade faded, and I could never be sure I saw the true Jax. I set up camp on the couch and she did the same on my bed, and we stayed in our respective zones when we were in the apartment. I found myself spending more time at the gym in the evenings than before, just to have something to do.

While we each stayed in our lanes, there was something comforting about having another person around. Someone to say "bless you" when you sneezed or to mix up a post-workout drink to be waiting when you returned from your self-exile exercise.

These gestures made me want to reach out in return, but every time I thought of something, Jax had already taken care of it. My anticipation-of-needs game needed some work.

The comfort of having Jax around extended to night time, even though we now slept in two different places. She always agreed to me turning the lights out, but the glow from her computer and clicking of keys filtered over my brown noise, typically lulling me right to sleep. But not tonight.

"You're not working on stuff for the senator late into the night, right?" I spoke into the darkness after an hour or so of failed sleep.

Jax let out a squeak. The sound of covers rustling made me think her computer slid off her lap. "I didn't know you were still awake."

I let out a low chuckle. "Sorry, didn't mean to startle you. But he's not working you this hard already, right?"

"Like someone's tenure would have any impact on the amount of work that man assigns you. But no, this isn't for the senator."

I waited a beat to see if she would continue. She didn't.

"Not going to share what you *are* working on?" I asked.

"No, I don't think I am. What are you still doing up? Don't you have to be at the airport in . . . wow, four hours? I didn't realize it was that late."

I nodded before I remembered she couldn't see me. "Yeah, ass crack of dawn is Mitchell's preferred time to travel. I just don't sleep well the night before a trip." This part of me stayed hidden from anyone outside my family. Telling Jax felt right somehow, like it might throw a grappling hook over one of her walls. I tentatively dangled a thread to sharing out there, wondering if Jax would take the bait.

She did. "Oh. Afraid you'll miss your alarm?"

"I'm pretty trained to snap awake to the sound of beeping at this point. I mentioned that my mom died when I was pretty young?"

Jax was quiet for a moment. "Yeah, I remember." Her voice was gentle.

"She had been sick for a while, but had been home from her latest hospital stay for a few weeks. My fifth-grade class was scheduled to take an overnight trip to visit the Boston aquarium. Both she and my dad really wanted me to go. It had been a hard time, and they wanted me to have some normalcy, I guess."

"And let me guess, you were super into sharks?"

I laughed. "I *was* super into sharks. How did you know?"

"Most ten-year-old boys are really into some sort of deadly animal at that age. I took a guess."

"But anyway, my mom died in her sleep that night, while I was on the trip. Logically, I know now that being home wouldn't have meant I got to say goodbye any differently than I had when giving her a kiss and hug before leaving for my trip. Ten-year-old me had a lot of trouble with that concept. It took a long time before I wanted to spend a night away from home, away from my brothers and dad."

"I'm sorry. I promise I know firsthand how empty those words can feel, but I really do mean it. My parents died in a car accident when I was thirteen. I went to live with my grandma, who was great, but died when I was in college. That feeling you have of never wanting to leave home? I . . . I guess I try to never get comfortable enough to call a place home."

The darkness enveloped us in relative silence. Ambient noise from the street and the brown noise app kept us from counting the breaths that passed until someone spoke again. Something about darkness made secrets slip out easily, gave you courage to let someone else see a part of who you really are.

"I have to ask," Jax said, breaking the quiet. "If you struggle so much with traveling and being away from home, why a politician? They spend half of their lives traveling."

An amused huff of air left me. I knew being a reporter wasn't Jax's true calling, but she had a knack for getting to the meat of an issue. "I promise, I'm a lot better than I used to be. Therapy helped some. Being a politician is because of my mom too, though. She was civically minded, always involved in helping her community and keeping up to date on elections and issues. She gave me my first Electoral College lesson, helping me color in the map red and blue after everyone else went to bed.

"And then after she died, we relied a lot on different community services to make ends meet. My dad was left with not only five sons to care for, but a mountain of medical debt too. That all sort of compounded into this desire to fight for others, make a difference. So here I am."

If anyone could see me, I knew my cheeks would be flushed pink. This may be the first time I ever told someone outside my family about the ties my mom had to my drive as a politician. What started as a desire to expose a bit of myself and gain back some of the distance Jax had put between us became a major share fest.

"That's what's going to make you one of the good ones. You're in it for the right reasons. But you should try to sleep. I imagine the senator is one of the working travelers, not much for sky naps." A click from Jax shutting her laptop traveled across the bookshelf separating us.

"You're not wrong about that. Thanks for listening."

"You're welcome," she whispered, as if talking in a loud voice would disturb me from dropping off.

I readjusted on the couch, finally feeling like sleep might not evade me. As my eyes grew heavier, I finally fell asleep.

All too soon, the beeping of my alarm sounded from the coffee table. I silenced it as quickly as I could and lay still, hoping I had cut it off before it woke Jax. Not hearing any movement from the bed, I quietly got up and headed to take a shower. I had laid the clothes I would need for the trip out the night before, and my packed bag waited by the door, trying to reduce disruptions at the ungodly hour.

The apartment was still too dark to make out anything beyond a covered lump in my bed in the corner as I prepared to meet the car scheduled to take me to the airport. I looked in that direction anyway, filled with something that tasted a lot like regret. Jax and I shared a lot of ourselves last night in those wee morning hours. I hated I would be gone for almost a week, worried the progress that sharing created would be washed away by the distance.

I closed the door behind me and made my way to the elevator, an idea taking hold. I texted Laurel with my plan, knowing her do not disturb settings meant her phone wouldn't ping at this absurd hour. Tucking my phone away, the strain of leaving reduced knowing something to look forward to waited for my return.

I hoped Jax would like my surprise. I thought of her voice in the darkness last night, the understanding, the empathy, the interest that bled into her side of the conversation. Hopefully she would be comfortable in the apartment with me gone this week. We hadn't really talked about it. I wondered if we'd talk while I was away.

As I slid into the car and set off for the airport, I realized I might have more than one thing to look forward to when I returned.

CHAPTER
Eleven

JAX

I lay still on the bed in the dark, waiting for the sound of the door closing behind Preston as he left for his trip. Our conversation from a few hours ago echoed in my mind. I couldn't remember the last time I willingly told someone about my parents dying. Preston respected the boundaries I erected all week, but something in the way he confessed his trouble sleeping before trips felt like an olive branch. I couldn't decide if what I felt at his departure was relief or sadness.

I threw the covers off the bed, grabbing my laptop, and made my way to the couch. The timing of Preston's trip couldn't be better. This book was due to my editor on Wednesday, and it needed work. My alpha readers, people I met online who only knew my pen name and not my face, mentioned they found the emotional connection between the two heroines lacking. Considering how much of this book had been scramble written under the cover of darkness while I listened to Preston snore softly just feet away, I wasn't terribly surprised. One of the hardest things about being an author sometimes was stepping outside yourself and not projecting on the pages how you felt at a given time.

With my computer in my lap, I dug into my manuscript. The light pouring in from the windows signaled several hours had passed without my notice. I stood up and stretched, realizing I was truly alone, and comfortable, in an apartment for the first time in a long time. Sure, other places I'd stayed emptied out when roommates traveled, but this was different

As a longtime subletter, I felt wanted in a place for the first time in years. More than Preston making room for my stuff when I moved in last week, he checked in on me, consciously or not. The combined grocery run put more food at my fingertips than I'd had in a long time. He clearly didn't know a FODMAP diet from a nutrition pyramid, but gamely asked me what I often ate for dinner, and adjusted accordingly. He made sure I ate all three meals, because we were together morning, noon, and night. I couldn't remember the last time I ate on such a regular schedule.

And if Preston noticed my occasional longer-than-normal bathroom trips, he didn't comment on them, just like he gamely used the bathroom spray I added to the back of the toilet each time he used the facilities too. If you were in Preston Brandt's orbit, he looked out for you. That's just the guy he was.

I made a promise to myself that I would try to keep up the habits of eating real food throughout the weekend. Per usual for this point in revisions though, my writing took over, and I ended up ordering delivery all weekend. By Monday morning, my book felt like less of a mess, but my stomach couldn't say the same.

"Morning, Jax," Laurel greeted me as I walked into the office that morning.

"Morning, Laurel," I responded. "Have a good weekend?"

"Not too bad. My cousin just moved to the city for a new job, so Caitlin and I helped her move. We discovered a fantastic happy hour just down the block from her place though. You'll have to come with us some time. No offense, but you look like you could use a margarita."

I blanched at the thought of adding tequila to my mixed-up

stomach. "I had a long weekend full of work on a personal project, that's all."

"Awe, not stressed because you're missing Preston?" she teased. It was a relief to have *someone* else know that things with Preston and I weren't real, but Laurel took advantage of this role at every turn.

I rolled my eyes, but then realized some truth lay in her question. "I miss his meal planning, that's for sure," I quipped, gripping my stomach in an exaggerated way that made Laurel laugh.

"Speaking of Preston, he's arranged a little something for us on Thursday evening. I'm supposed to tell you to clear your schedule."

I blinked, a little taken aback. Why wouldn't he just tell me himself? I realized then that Preston and I hadn't talked since he left Saturday morning. Did that make me a failure as a fake fiancée? I wasn't sure.

"I'm not sure Thursday evening is good for me. I have this big deadline on Wednesday and . . ."

"It has to be Thursday," Laurel cut me off. "The good thing about Senator Marsden and Preston being gone until then is the office will be quiet and distraction free. You'll definitely finish anything he left you in plenty of time, maybe even be able to get ahead."

I didn't bother correcting her it wasn't senatorial comms stuff I was concerned about. It seemed like there was no getting out of the mandated date night on Thursday.

"All right, Thursday. I've got it noted. I'd better get to it then. Those responses to the weekend talk shows aren't going to write themselves."

Laurel waved and got back to her own work, the phone ringing as I walked down the hallway to my desk. I sat down, turned on my computer, but pulled my phone out before getting right to work.

JAX

So Thursday? What are you up to, Brandt?

I started going through my email while I waited for him to answer.

PRESTON

It's a surprise. I'll meet you in the office at 5:45, okay? We land at DCA at 5:00. Send good travel vibes, please.

JAX

Anything I should know about a dress code?

PRESTON

Whatever you wear to work will be fine.

Well, that was nothing to go on. Maybe I could get Laurel to spill more details over the next few days. It would be nice to have something to celebrate handing off another book. It was lonely having a secret pen name, no one to share in your accomplishments. I opened the shared folder to start crafting statements when my phone buzzed on my desk again.

PRESTON

On second thought, wear something blue. It'll bring out your eyes.

Was my fake fiancé flirting with me? Certainly not.

Shaking my head, I put my phone on silent and got to work. Laurel wasn't wrong. It should be easy to get through tasks today without the guys in the office. If I could sneak out early and get back to my book, it wouldn't be the worst thing.

Wednesday night, I sent my finished manuscript to my editor at nine and promptly passed out until the next morning. I woke up to three texts from Preston.

PRESTON

Did you see this?
www.youtube.com/x7tU8LmP

I clicked on the link and saw the trailer for the new season of Survivor. I learned this week through texts that Preston binged old seasons in the evening, but only while he traveled, like a real weirdo.

PRESTON

The champions seasons are never my favorite, mostly because they give me the urge to cross reference their original seasons. It's exhausting.

Please forget I ever told you that. It's embarrassing and you could use it to jettison my future campaign if things between us go south.

I laughed out loud. Texts between Preston and I had regained that jokey cadence we'd lost after the couch purchasing incident. My stomach gave a nervous twinge at the thought of tonight. I presumed whatever his big surprise turned out to be would involve lights and encourage talking face-to-face. Preston Brandt was getting under my skin. There was no doubt about it.

My stomach twisted again, this time alerting me that nature was calling. This week had reached a point where anything I ate made me sick, no matter how safe it normally was for my system. Sometimes when I reached this stage, careful eating helped me get back on track. Other times, like this week, I entered a fuck it phase, and ate whatever sounded good and was convenient. As I cleansed the bathroom of this most recent encounter, I fully realized the error of that choice, given Preston would be back in this apartment with me tonight. Hopefully I could snap my system out of it with small meals and bland food choices.

The day turned out to be a real shitstorm in the professional realm as well. At his final campaign stop last night, Senator Marsden got into a shouting match with an opposition voter who interrupted his speech. Damage control took precedence most of the day, and we were scrambling to keep up with normal daily tasks.

"It's after five, you know. You don't have to be working so diligently. Senator Marsden is off on an emergency two-hour session with his kickboxing instructor, which should lull him to sleep for six hours, instead of his usual four."

I smiled at my desk at the sound of Preston's voice. Without looking up from the document I was editing, I said, "That's rich coming from the man who admitted to regularly staying at the office past seven before he went and got himself engaged." The smile widened as I took him in, all tall and handsome in his suit, leaning against the wall. His posture read tired, but his eyes sparkled.

"Birds of a feather, I guess," he said, returning my smile.

"Guys, let's goooo," Laurel whined, appearing next to him. "Caitlin's already there waiting for us and you know how long the line gets if you get there too long past six. I *need* a drink after today."

I grabbed my coat and bag, following them out of the office. "I don't know how long the line gets. Where are we going?"

"You'll see," Preston answered mysteriously before Laurel could get a word out.

We entered the tunnel like we were heading back to the Capitol from the Russell Building, but then took a turn I hadn't noticed before. I looked all around, trying to guess which direction we were headed, hoping they weren't actually going to murder me as part of the second week on the job hazing.

"The Library of Congress?" I asked, as we started climbing a set of stairs at the end of the tunnel. A sign overhead showed our arrival at the building. "But isn't it closed? It's after five."

"It's Live! at the Library on Thursdays," Laurel explained excitedly. "You get to be in the building after dark. They still do the tours and such, but there are adult beverages and music. It's fun."

We walked through the metal detectors and checked our coats and bags. I took in the marble and architecture of the building, craning my neck every which way. We climbed another set of stairs to the main level, where a crowd of people waited in line in the central open area, under the painted ceiling.

"Bless her. She got in line when I told her we were walking over. Let's go." Laurel led the way toward a pretty black woman in a red dress and tights, giving her a peck as she stepped close. "Caitlin, this is Jax, Preston's *fiancée* I was telling you about." The emphasis on the word gave away that Caitlin also knew the truth.

"It's nice to meet you," I said, holding out my hand to shake hers. "I can only imagine the energy this one brings into a home, considering how she is at the office."

"I'm a fucking delight, thank you," Laurel said, snaking her arm around Caitlin's waist. "Plus, my energy means I'm great in bed."

Caitlin looked at Laurel adoringly before meeting my eyes and muttering from the side of her mouth, "She's not wrong."

We all laughed. Preston asked Caitlin about her job at a human rights law firm. That conversation kept us occupied until our turn to order drinks came around.

"Just water for me," I said to the woman looking at me expectantly.

"Wait," Laurel interjected. "I'm not meaning to be a booze pusher if you really don't want a drink, but didn't you say you had a big deadline yesterday? Do you want something to celebrate? We can toast, and you can tell us what it was?"

I looked at Preston who shrugged. I turned back to the

bartender, who looked a little less patient than she had thirty seconds ago. "I'll take a Prosecco, please."

Laurel was right. I did want to take this opportunity to celebrate with my new friends. I hadn't eaten much today, but my stomach had been fairly stable since this morning. One glass shouldn't hurt.

We sipped our drinks on the mezzanine level, leaning against the banisters and people watching. Laurel and Caitlin seemed to know half the people here tonight, someone always coming and going, saying hi, offering plans for the weekend, or extending an invite to some dinner or another.

Preston leaned down to mutter in my ear. "I've never felt like a collective third wheel before."

I laughed softly, as I nodded in welcome to yet someone else stepping up to say hello. "Who knew your coworker was so popular?"

"Not me," he answered. He nodded at my empty glass. "Do you want another drink?"

I glanced at the line and took stock of the effect of the bubbles reaching my head on a mostly empty stomach. "No, I think I'm good."

He took my glass out of my hand and tossed it in a nearby trashcan. "Let's go wait in line to walk through the reading room, then? The only problem with happy hour is so many of the exhibits are food and drink free." He extended his elbow, and I threaded my hand through it. Ever the doting fiancé, at least while we were in public.

We chatted about his trip and he caught me up on the Survivor drama he watched this week, even though I had no idea who he was talking about. Soon, we were ushered forward and walked into the reading room. The size and grandness of the room struck me. The dome ceiling rose over the multiple floors of stacks, while chairs created individual workstations facing either the center of the circular room or the shelves of books.

The hush of the room promised productivity and enlightenment, just by the vibes of the space.

Preston gently propelled me forward as the people behind us crowded in where I had stopped still.

"I should come here and write," I muttered.

"What's that?" he asked quietly as we completed our too quick circuit and exited the room.

"Oh, just imagining what it would be like to work in that room. Seems pretty quiet."

"Definitely no senator outbursts, needy interns, or Laurels distracting you in that room. I think it's pretty easy to apply for a card during business hours."

I looked longingly over my shoulder. I wish we could have stayed longer.

"Come on, there's an overlook where you can take it in uninterrupted." Preston jerked his head toward a marble staircase leading to large glass panes overlooking the reading room.

We started heading that way when I saw a familiar face in the crowd.

"Fuck," I said as I grabbed Preston's arm and pulled him to the side of the stairs.

"What's wrong?" he asked, his head swiveling around in concern.

"That's that devil woman over at *The Dispatch* who got me fired." I leaned out from behind Preston and noticed her heading right for us.

I looked around and noticed a little alcove underneath the stairs next to us. I pulled Preston with me, leaning my back against the wall, my eyes closed. Maybe I overreacted slightly at the sight of my nemesis. I landed on my feet okay, but like I told the senator, I wasn't convinced she wouldn't come after me again. Avoiding her seemed easier.

"Want to tell me what that was all about?" Preston's voice sounded from directly above me. I realized I still held onto his arm with a death grip and had pulled him flush against me in my fervor to get out of sight.

I looked up at my fake fiancé, taking my time to examine his features up close. The way his brow furrowed in concern at my worry. The fullness of his bottom lip. The flecks of brown and gold in his hazel eyes. The way those eyes were on my mouth.

"Jax?" he asked, his arm finding its way to the wall next to my head, as if he needed help standing.

"No," I said, before pulling his head down, crushing his lips to mine. Almost just as quickly, he pulled his head back.

"No?" he asked, the confusion clear on his face.

"No, to telling you what's going on. Yes, to the kissing," I answered, throwing all caution to the wind.

Whether I could thank the adrenaline of spotting Peggy in the crowd or the feeling of a live wire lighting up my body when Preston's lips met mine, any residual effects of the wine fled. Preston slid his arm from my grip, wrapping it around my lower back. He arched my hips into his as he deepened the kiss.

My shoulders dug into the wall behind me, even as he supported us with the hand above my head as he leaned in. I moved my hands up his chest, looping one around his neck to return the pressure, while the other tangled in his hair. Our mouths moved together, fiery and tender all at once, as we mapped each other's lips. Preston groaned into my mouth, which I took as an invitation to tangle my tongue with his.

Then, two things happened almost simultaneously. First, the service elevator to my left chimed. The doors rattled open, revealing our tender embrace in a private spot at a very public event. Second, my stomach cramped threateningly, letting me know punishment lingered only moments away.

Preston stepped back when the elevator doors opened, running his hand across his mouth. A Library of Congress employee stood there looking amused. I slid to the side, out from between Preston and the wall, straightening my dress.

"I, uh, I need to go. You should find Laurel and Caitlin. I'll see you back at your place. Later."

I turned and nodded at the employee with as much dignity as I could and started walking toward the edge of the room, searching for the bathroom I noted when we walked in.

"Jax, wait," Preston called from behind me, but I slipped into a group of visitors exiting the reading room, dodging this way and that to cut through the crowd, leaving him behind.

I locked the stall door behind me and put my face in my hands. *What the* hell *was that?*

CHAPTER
Twelve

PRESTON

I ran my hand through my hair as I searched the crowded room for any signs of brown hair and a royal blue dress. I absent-mindedly raised my hand to my lips again, reliving the best kiss of my life. Damn that elevator. But also, where did she *go?*

I pulled out my phone and dialed Jax's number when I heard my name called from behind me. Laurel and Caitlin made their way toward me as Jax's voicemail clicked on. "Leave a message at the beep. Or you know, text me. It's not the '90s."

I suppressed a growl as the couple reached me.

"Where did you guys go?" Laurel asked. "I thought maybe you left."

"We went through the reading room, and then . . . Have you guys seen Jax?"

Laurel looked at me like I was an easily spooked cat. "No, like I just said, we weren't sure where you went or if you were still here."

I nodded. "Right. I lost track of Jax a minute ago. She told me she'd see me back at home, but I feel weird leaving her here."

Laurel shrugged. "I get the vibes Jax has been taking care of herself for a long time. If she tells you to leave, I think you can leave. And you know, with your arrangement, I don't actually think it's a trap."

Caitlin laughed. "Women," I muttered, lifting my phone to call her again. Voicemail. Damn it.

"Are you okay?" Laurel asked, that look of concern in her eyes again.

"Yeah, I'm fine. We were just . . . and then she was . . . and now I can't . . ." I couldn't seem to complete a thought. Jax's mouth and then sudden absence of her entire being scrambled my brain.

"We'll keep an eye out for her until we leave and let you know if we see her. Maybe you should go home and see if she somehow beat you there?" Caitlin suggested, her look mirroring Laurel's. I must be giving off a real wild energy.

I nodded. "Okay, yeah, that's a good plan." This place was too big and had too many stairwells to the exit. I could stay here and wait for her, and still miss her leaving.

I walked down to the coat check, still swiveling my head, keeping an eye out for Jax. I handed over my number, trying to see if I could recognize Jax's coat next to where the clerk grabbed mine. This was late-winter in DC though. The coat-room was full of a hundred black pea coats and nothing stood out.

I called Jax again as I left the building, with no answer. At the edge of the steps leading down to First Street, the Capitol lit up across from me, I stopped to decide whether I wanted to take a car home or burn off some energy with a walk. My phone vibrated in my hand, interrupting my pondering, and I saw a text from Jax. I jabbed at the phone to open it.

JAX

Oh my god, Brandt, I'm fine. Just needed a
bathroom ASAP and am not sure how long I'll
be here. I'll see you at your place.

I stared at the phone, wondering why she hadn't said so

earlier. Considering how we met, and that we lived together, it wasn't like I didn't know about her digestive trouble.

PRESTON

I'm just outside, I can wait.

JAX

Someone waiting on me makes it worse.
You've been away for almost a week. Just go,
I'll be fine.

I let out a frustrated huff. This woman. One minute I was kissing her under a staircase in a library, the next she shut me out.

PRESTON

Can I get you anything?

I waited for a few minutes to no response. I guess that meant no. I started to walk home, sending one more message.

PRESTON

Promise me you'll call a car at least?

JAX

Okay.

I jammed my phone in my jacket pocket, my hands following against the cold bite in the air, my breath visible in front of me. Crossing the street, I hurried my steps toward my apartment. I turned on Pennsylvania and saw a convenience store ahead. With my mind made up, I entered the store. I had no idea what I would grab, but I would not return to my apartment empty handed.

Jax somehow managed to beat me home, between my stop for supplies and relying on my feet to get me there. I took that to mean she listened to me and took a car home.

"How are you?" I called through the closed bathroom door, heading to the kitchen to unload my supplies.

A groan answered me. "Can you turn the TV on or something? Please?"

As an only child, Jax didn't understand growing up with four brothers made you immune to sound effects, but it was a reasonable request, so I didn't argue.

I asked Alexa to play my Daylist on Spotify. Cottage rock acoustic rainy nighttime music, or something with an equally ridiculous theme, started to play. My suitcase sat tucked next to the dresser, where I dropped it earlier before meeting Jax and Laurel at the office. I picked it up, intending to set it on the bed, like I usually did to unpack after a trip. I paused with the suitcase in the air, realizing the bed belonged to Jax now. Should I use it as a resting spot for my dirty luggage?

"Even if you were living here alone, you're asking to bring bed bugs home with that habit," Jax said, correctly reading my intentions from across the room. She walked to the couch and threw herself down. Clearly, she had no trouble making herself comfortable in the space while I was gone.

I set the suitcase back on the floor. She had a point.

"I, uh, got you some stuff," I said, abandoning the idea of unpacking in favor of grabbing a Gatorade and sleeve of Saltines from the kitchen area. Jax looked at me speculatively as I walked over, offering them to her.

"I don't have the flu, you know."

I set the bottle and crackers down on the table harder than necessary before bringing my hands to my hips.

"Well, I didn't know what to do. One second you were kissing the crap out of me, and the next you were just gone. I couldn't just do *nothing*. I don't do helpless well."

Jax crossed her arms, leaning back into the couch cushions, her face set in defiance.

"Well, I don't do damsel in distress well."

"Seriously? The day this"—I gestured between us—"all started, you were very much in dist—"

"Okay, okay. That's fair. I suppose I should say I don't do vulnerable well. You've already helped me in this type of situation once. I knew we were coming back to the same place, and as you said, I was kissing the crap out of you. Nice choice of words, by the way." She raised her eyebrow as my phrasing hit me.

Jax's eyes crinkled at the corners and she started to laugh. I joined her, in part at my unintentional joke and another to let out the joy that bubbled in my gut at seeing her laugh.

I plopped myself onto the other edge of the sofa. "So, you're okay?"

Jax leaned forward and took the Gatorade off the table, twisting off the cap to take a few large swallows.

"I'm okay. And sorry I bit your head off about the supplies. It's sweet and hydrating isn't a bad idea." She started to mess with the wrapper on the bottle, avoiding my eyes.

"You're welcome."

We sat in silence for a few moments.

"So, about that kiss," I said.

"I think that security guard might win this week's story telling competition," she said. "But I don't think it should happen again."

I absorbed her words, my emotions warring. On one hand, I knew she had a point. We were *fake* engaged, and our quarters were just too tight 24/7 to add anything physical. But, on the other hand, the one I used solely in the shower since Jax moved in, I wanted to kiss those lips again. And then the rest of her.

"It's just that we're on top of each other—figuratively, that is —all the time, and I think it's playing with fire to let anything get physical when it's just us. I know we'll still need to touch in public," she continued when I didn't say anything.

I nodded slowly. "I see your point. But it *was* some kiss, am I right?"

Jax didn't answer me, pushing herself into a standing position. "I'm going to take a shower and then turn in early."

"Do you want anything for dinner? I can see what we have. If not, I might go to the gym."

Jax shook her head. "I think Saltines and Gatorade for dinner will be perfect."

She gathered what she needed for her shower while I stared straight ahead, trying to make myself get up and go to the gym. I was vaguely aware of the bathroom door opening and closing and the water turning on when I heard the door open again.

"Preston?" Jax stuck her head out of the door. "It was a hell of a kiss."

At that, she shut the door again and presumably carried on with her shower. I got ready for the gym with what I knew was a huge grin on my face. My boppiest playlist playing in my ears, I pounded away on the treadmill. Maybe I shouldn't, but I couldn't help looking forward to falling asleep in the same room as my fake fiancée later.

CHAPTER
Thirteen

PRESTON

Jax and I slid into a more comfortable co-existence following our night at the Library of Congress. Did that involve me being more physically aware of her whenever we shared a room? It did. But this familiar, if platonic, version of our relationship was preferable to the strained version from before.

"Preston, I need the speech for the Young Liberal's fund dinner. And also pass the lo mein."

"I'll have it for you in five," I answered while pushing the white carton across the coffee table.

The primary elections in Rhode Island were in ten days, and we hadn't left the office before seven all week. Even liaising with the campaign team seemed to take longer than normal. I couldn't imagine what things would have been like if Jax hadn't been around.

Her genius wasn't limited to the office. We currently were trying to cram a Saturday's worth of work into Friday evening at home so we could have a day off tomorrow. The weather forecast predicted a sixty-degree day and sunshine. The spring thaw had officially arrived in Washington, DC.

"Okay, sent. I think that's it."

"Knock on wood right now, Brandt. Open a file or your email, quick," she responded, not even bothering to look over at me.

I smiled, bringing up my email inbox, not wanting to close my computer until Jax was finished with the speech I just sent her. There were always emails to answer.

She slammed the lid of her laptop moments later and threw it onto the couch next to her, stretching with a groan. "Okay, done. Are you sure we have to go outside tomorrow and enjoy the weather? Staying in bed all day, watching the sun from inside, also sounds pretty great."

My phone buzzed from the table, distracting me from images of staying in bed with Jax all day. I needed to cool it. Duncan's name flashed on the screen. I debated ignoring it, but if he was actually calling, he wouldn't give up until he talked to me.

"Hey, Dunc, Happy Friday. What's up?"

"Just calling to confirm you and your lovely fiancée you've managed to share very few details about will be at the Brandt Investing International cleanup day at the river tomorrow."

I managed to stifle a groan. I completely forgot I agreed to help with BII's community service day tomorrow.

"Oh yup, we'll be there. It's been on our minds all week."

Jax's head whipped in my direction, mouthing, "What?" I shook my head at her, but clicked my phone on speaker so she could hear. "Jax is here now, actually."

"I'd really think someone with your political aspirations would be better at lying by now, Prez," Duncan said, pulling out my family nickname. Jax's eyes lit up with glee and I cringed, sure I'd never live that one down.

"We'll be there, no doubt. What time again?"

I could almost hear Duncan roll his eyes. "I had my assistant email you the details five minutes ago. Remember, you, Laurel, and now the lovely Jax are on bagel duty."

This time the groan slipped out as I slumped on the couch, my head lying on the back cushions. Duncan had corralled

Laurel and Caitlin into volunteering too, months ago, when he came up to the office with me to pick something up.

"See you both at 7:00 a.m. Don't be late." The glee in his voice was just cruel.

I hung up without saying goodbye, though regretted it a second later, and sent a "Night, Dunc" text. He acknowledged with a thumbs up shortly after.

"So, we're cleaning up a river tomorrow? With your brother?"

I rolled my head so I was looking in her direction. "At least we'll be outside in the nice weather?"

She laughed at my pain. "I'll need to find something that looks fiancée-like with my galoshes. I'll definitely want to be sure to leave the ring behind."

I scrubbed my hands over my face, picking my phone up to text Laurel and hope she had remembered bagels.

"So, tell me what I need to know for tomorrow. I'm honestly surprised we've made it this long without another brother run-in."

I pushed myself up and grabbed the picture of the five of us from a barbecue at Dad and Margaret's house two summers ago.

I pointed to the photo. "You met Hayden at the fundraiser."

She nodded. "And his girlfriend is Charlotte, who works with bookstores. What does he do? Will she be there?"

I smiled at her thoroughness, then I frowned. Maybe we should have been doing this all along—it was a lot to keep track of in one night.

"Right now, Hayden works for Duncan, but he's leaving soon to form his own consulting firm under the umbrella of Duncan's company. He works in IT and wants to help start-ups with their technology. And yes, I would bet Charlotte will be there. It's looking to be a whole family affair. Hunter"—I pointed at the picture again—"Hayden's twin, is in town this weekend too. Uncertain if that was scheduled before or after Duncan roped us all into this cleanup."

"And what does Hunter do?"

I paused for a beat. "Hunter is a bit of a wanderer. He's still searching for his calling, moving from job to job. I may have mentioned he lives in Holly Ridge, where Dad and Margaret live, but he finally got his own place a few years ago. I think that was good for him."

Jax nodded again, taking a turn to point at the picture. "And so that is Duncan, the oldest and protector of rivers." I laughed, picturing Duncan's face if Jax ever called him a tree hugger. "And that," she continued, "is Spencer, the baby. He's doing something academic, right?"

I looked over at her. She shrugged. "You talk about them more than you think you do. I had vague pieces of the puzzle, but figured this was the time to bring it all into focus."

I nodded, trying to hide my shock. My brothers were important to me, but it was rare that I shared them with people right away. They were precious relationships, ones I didn't expose easily.

"All right. Well, I think that should cover it. I'm pretty good at going with the flow and uncovering connections as they unveil themselves. We should take care of this"—she nodded to the chaos filled coffee table in front of us—"and get to sleep. The river calls and we must go."

I stood, gathering the remnants of our dinner as Jax grabbed our laptops and put them next to the TV, out of the way. The containers filled up the small kitchen trash can, so after rinsing the dishes, I grabbed the bag to take it to the trash chute by the elevators.

When I returned, Jax was climbing into bed, her face clean and hair piled on top of her head. She settled under the covers.

"Hey," I said, standing awkwardly in the middle of the room. "Thanks for rolling with it, and being willing to go tomorrow. I'm sure it's not your ideal Saturday, but it means a lot."

Jax shrugged, but a small smile turned up her lips. "I know it's not easy for you to lie to your family about our relationship. Me refusing to go would make you lie even more and probably create a lot of questions. Besides, how a person acts around his family can tell you a lot about them. I'm having fun figuring you out, Brandt."

With that, she rolled over, pulling the blankets tight up to her neck. Her words bounced in my head as I brushed my teeth and got my couch bed situated before turning off the lights. Just as I tucked myself in, I heard Jax's voice, muffled into her pillow.

"Don't forget to see if Laurel confirmed about the bagels. See you at 5:30."

I grabbed my phone and saw confirmation from Laurel she had placed a bagel order weeks ago, along with a quip about men being helpless.

"She's on it. Night, Jax."

Sometimes, it wasn't so bad to have someone in your corner backing you up. I fell asleep smiling.

The smile disappeared as I stood along the banks of the Anacostia River along the Anacostia River Trail as the sun was brightening the sky.

"Here, have a bagel, grumpy Gus," Jax said, handing me one with plenty of cream cheese, just the way I liked it. "Aren't you supposed to be the morning person in this relationship?"

"Hmph," I said, biting into my bagel, the taste of the everything seasoning and creamy filling lifting my spirits a bit.

"There he is," Jax teased, her eyes focusing on something behind me. "Incoming," she muttered.

"Well, if it isn't our love birds."

I turned around to face my older brother, somehow still looking very much like a CEO in work pants and boots. It must be all in the posture.

"Hi, Duncan, it's great to meet you." Jax stuck out her hand, which Duncan accepted, his raised eyebrow indicating he was impressed.

"Likewise, Jax. I'd say I'm sure we would have met sooner, but I was out of the country. Though since none of us knew you existed until that ring was on your finger, I'm not so sure that's the truth." Duncan pinned me with a glance. Sometimes he forgot he wasn't actually our father, even though he had helped out a ton to raise us while Dad worked after Mom died.

"Can we not do this right—"

"That's on me." Jax cut me off with a hand on my arm. "I have some personal things surrounding family, and I asked Preston if we could wait to broaden our circle for a while."

Both of us looked at her, me in surprise that she would sprinkle some of her personal truth around the lie she weaved to get Duncan off my back. Duncan's eyes showed respect. He valued someone who took ownership and didn't shrink in the face of adversity.

"I can appreciate that. We just want to meet who each other is serious about, especially Preston after—"

"Oh, look at that, it's Hayden and Charlotte and Hunter," I exclaimed, cutting Duncan off and shooting him a glare. We were *not* going to talk about my past relationship on the side of the river.

We all exchanged handshakes and hugs, me holding Hunter for a second longer than necessary. I didn't get to see him much, and I worried, but he didn't like to know that. So an extra-long hug was the best I could do to let him know I had his back.

Hunter eventually pushed me away, sticking his hand out to Jax. "So you're the gal who finally got my brother to thaw his heart again, huh? Great to meet you."

I groaned as Jax and Hunter shook hands. Jax raised an eyebrow at me, but the organizer of the cleanup yelled for everyone's attention and saved me from having to respond.

After we broke into groups, each covering a different part of the trail, I held my hand on Jax's arm to hold her back from our team slightly.

"Hey, about what Hunter said," I started.

She shook her head. "It's fine, Preston. I'm not an idiot. You had a ring ready with your mother's jewelry in it. There's obviously a story there. If things were *different*, I hope you'd tell me." She glanced around making sure none of my family was in earshot. "But since they're not. It's okay. I don't need to know." She smiled at me and walked away to catch up with Charlotte, the two of them falling into quick conversation about some new romance novel as they stabbed at trash along the ground.

Duncan came up behind me, clapping his hand on my shoulder. "I like her. I think she's good for you."

I looked up at him in surprise, because of course the asshole was the tallest in the family, and the richest. "You barely talked to her. You, Mister-background-checks-his-Tinder-dates, like her?"

"It's not Tinder. It's a dating app for men of means, and I don't do background checks on them, the app does. But *anyway*, yes, I like her. She stood up for you, and she's here, facing all of this." He gestured to our family with his own stick. I considered his words. One of Duncan's biggest problems with Diana, my ex, had always been that she never showed up. Jax did more than that for a fake relationship.

"And besides," he said, walking toward the rest of the group. "You can't keep your eyes off her."

CHAPTER
Fourteen

JAX

Spending three hours cleaning up trash may not have been how I imagined spending my Saturday off, but I had to admit to feeling refreshed from the fresh air. Preston's brothers were entertaining, and Charlotte and I could talk about books for hours. Not the worst way to spend a day off, plus we gathered a ton of trash from along the walking path.

I bent over to touch my toes, stretching out my back, waiting for our host to officially dismiss us.

"Dude, ogle your fiancée's ass in public a little less. There are kids around."

I stood up and turned around to find Preston's cheeks flushed pink and Hunter wearing a shit-eating grin. I smiled and walked over to the brothers. I leaned toward Preston's ear, intentionally choosing the side Hunter stood on and said, "Why look when you can touch?" in a low voice.

To my delight, Preston's cheeks got darker before he got a determined look in his eye. He slid his arm down my back, resting his hand on my ass. To my surprise, he slid my puffy vest and long-sleeve tee up my back slightly before hooking his thumb into the waistband of my yoga pants.

My shirt moved back down, covering his wandering thumb, which he proceeded to slide back and forth over the sliver of skin he had exposed. My breath caught, surprised to find my lower back, or more accurately, upper ass, to be such an erogenous zone. A pleased smirk crossed Preston's face before he returned his attention to Hunter.

"So what's next?" Preston asked, pulling on the hand tucked into my pants so I had no choice but to step back next to him. I kept what I hoped was a normal smile on my face, while most of my attention focused on the two inches of flesh my fake fiancé kept stroking.

"What do you think, Jax?" Laurel, who apparently had joined our group in the past few minutes since my world was centered on a thumb, asked me.

"Oh, yeah, sounds great," I said, not wanting to give away how distracted I was.

She clapped her hands in glee. "Great, girls' brunch! We're meeting my cousin too. I think you guys will get along great."

I looked up at Preston. "I guess I'm going to girls' brunch."

Preston removed his hand and smiled knowingly at me. "I guess so. We're going to brunch too, it turns out. You would have been invited, but Charlotte can't come either, so now the brothers have an opportunity to grill me about our engagement. Thanks a lot." He smiled at me to lessen the sting of his words. I could tell in his eyes he was excited to spend time with his brothers, even if it meant time in the hot seat.

"Well, I guess I'll see you back at the apartment then." I found myself looking between Preston's lips and his eyes. Would his brothers expect us to kiss goodbye? In the early morning fogginess, having this conversation after our library make out last week hadn't crossed my mind.

"I guess so," Preston said, his eyes doing their own bouncing, a question in them.

I nodded slightly, and Preston leaned down to place a gentle peck on my lips before pulling away. He walked toward his brothers and Hayden threw his arm around Preston's neck as they set off toward their next stop.

Laurel came to stand next to me as I watched them walk away. "So, it's a good thing brunch includes mimosas, right?"

I looked over at her, catching the knowing look in her eye.

"I think I'm going to need a few. Hold the juice."

"Pretty sure we can make that happen." Laurel laughed and looped her arm through mine, leading me over to where Caitlin waited by their car.

The temperature finally cracked sixty degrees by the time we reached the restaurant. Between the plentiful sunshine and no breeze, it was a perfect day to sit outside and we were lucky enough to snag the last four top in Shaw's Tavern's outdoor dining section.

"Hi, Penny. We're all going to take bottomless mimosas and some bread for the table, please," Laurel said, as our waitress came over to greet us.

"Three for bottomless mimosas?" Penny confirmed with a smile. A busboy appeared, as if by magic, dropping off a basket of bread and olive oil for dipping.

"Make that four," a voice came from behind us, and Laurel stood up to hug a tall, beautiful redhead. The newcomer wore jeans and a blazer, putting us to shame in our river cleanup garb.

"Four it is," Penny said with a smile, walking away to put in our orders.

"Michelle, this is my new coworker, Jax. Jax, meet Michelle, my cousin, who's new to DC."

Michelle waved at me from across the table as she grabbed a slice of bread. "Hi, Jax. My cousin here tells me we should be friends. I'm not sure if she means that or if she's just sick of being the only person I know in the city outside of work."

"Hi," I answered. "Well, she tells me you live by a place with great margaritas, so as long as you like tequila, I think we'll be fast friends."

Michelle laughed. "Tequila and tacos, the foundation for any true friendship."

We made small talk, Michelle answering questions from Caitlin and Laurel about settling in and how her first week of work had gone.

Michelle heaved a heavy sigh. "It's fine. My boss called me in yesterday to tell me I needed to tone down the technical talk in my forecasts. Apparently, we've gotten some complaints."

"Michelle's the new meteorologist for KUSN, Channel Four" Caitlin said to me quietly, filling in context as Penny delivered a bottle of champagne and a few carafes of juice, plus glasses of water all around.

Michelle continued, champagne flute in the air. "My forecasts aren't that different from how some of the guys from Capital Weather Gang give them, but I guess because I'm a woman, people are viewing me as uptight and elitist."

I snorted. "Throw a stone in this town and you'll hit an elitist." And took a sip of my own drink. Champagne with just a splash of juice, the perfect brunch companion.

She raised her glass toward me. "That's part of why I took the job in this market. I figured I could deliver a unique brand of forecasting and it would fit here. But I guess not." She slumped back in her chair and emptied her glass. "Oh well, that's Monday's problem. What's up with you ladies?"

Caitlin talked about the case her firm had settled, and Laurel filled her in on some of the senator's latest antics. I chimed in here and there, but was content to take in the menu and enjoy the sunshine.

"But Jax here has fiancé problems, don't you, Jax?"

I snapped my head up and glared at Laurel, my eyes narrowing as she took in my delighted face. "No, I don't."

"Oh, I think you do," Caitlin chimed in as Laurel cackled. I debated whether I was too hungry to actually get up and leave right now, but then Penny arrived to take our food orders. I decided it might not be the worst thing in the world to get some outside perspective on the thoughts pinging around my brain.

"I'll have the waffles and a side of eggs, please. No cheese." I handed Penny my menu and poured myself a fresh drink from the bottle she delivered moments ago.

"So, Michelle. I know we just met, but can you keep a secret?"

Laurel clapped, bouncing in her seat as her cousin looked at me, confused.

"Is the secret that you're having fiancé problems? But yes, I can. A weather person is only as good as their trustworthy reputation." Michelle rolled her eyes at herself, letting me know she didn't take herself too seriously, but was game to keep my confidences.

"So, my engagement is fake," I started.

"But her lust is very real," Laurel finished.

"That's not quite how I was going to phrase it, but thank you."

"And how does he—oh, sorry," Michelle corrected herself. "Or she, or they, I shouldn't assume, feel about you?"

I laughed. "Sorry, I just remembered the last woman I dated —before Preston—broke up with me because I wasn't marriage material, but here I am, with a fiancé. Take that, Britney!" I swigged more of my drink before reaching for the glass of water Penny smartly brought for each of us. I should slow down until after I ate something. "I'm not really sure how he feels. He did refer to our kiss at the Library of Congress as 'some kiss.'"

Laurel gasped. "I *knew* something was up with him when he couldn't find you. Oh man, this is good. I've never seen Preston lose his head over a woman before. Tell me everything."

"There's not much to tell. We hid from my nemesis underneath the stairs, made out a little, and got interrupted by a poorly timed elevator door opening and my digestive system."

"Well, did you talk about it afterward?" Caitlin asked, leaning forward, clearly as invested as everyone else at the table.

"We did. I said I didn't think it was a good idea for us to be physical outside of instances where it was necessary to keep up appearances."

"And did he agree?" Michelle asked, eyeing me appraisingly.

"I think so?" I thought back to the conversation. "At the very least, he didn't argue with me."

We paused our conversation so the runner could deliver our plates.

"Well, if putting his hand on your ass in a public park before noon on a Saturday is keeping up appearances, then I have greatly underestimated Preston's game," Laurel said, digging into her breakfast scramble.

"His thumb might have sort of been inside my pants too," I muttered, concentrating on pouring syrup in each square of my waffle until Laurel gasped and dropped her silverware on the plate.

"Preston Brandt," she said, applauding lightly. "Who knew you had it in you?"

"Okay, while a bit extreme for appearance's sake, that doesn't actually tell us anything," Caitlin said, her lawyer voice firmly in place. "Jax, do you *want* Preston?"

I looked at each woman in turn, and voiced to them the truth I had been trying to hide from myself. "I do," I nodded. "I want to climb him like a tree."

"Ha!" Michelle exclaimed, her hand coming down on the table, causing a few people to look our way. She lowered her voice. "Laurel's right. We are going to be great friends. Climb him like a tree. I'm going to use that." She pulled out her phone.

"Sounds like someone else has some news they've been with-holding," Laurel said, watching her cousin.

"Just another form of stress relief," Michelle said, typing on her phone. "I downloaded Tinder last night on a whim." Laurel looked shocked. "I know, I know. Casual hook-ups are totally not my style, but that conversation with my boss really had me questioning a lot about myself last night. I went to delete it just as quickly, but got a message from a guy right away. RidgeMan93. He has lots of tattoos, abs I'd like to eat stuff off, and he's only in town for the weekend. New city, new me, right?"

Laurel didn't look so sure, but Caitlin kicked me on her way to tap Laurel's foot across the table. Laurel seemed to swallow what she was going to say, opting for, "Well, if you do meet up with him, make sure to share your location and keep me posted, okay?"

Michelle nodded. "Of course. He may not even answer. He said he had family stuff to do today and would see if he could get away. Now, back to you, Jax. What are you going to do about it?"

I thought for a moment and then looked over at Laurel. "Is there somewhere near here I could buy a new little *something* special? I think it's time to seduce my fiancé."

Laurel looked thrilled. "I know just the place. Let's go shopping."

CHAPTER
Fifteen

We made the trek across most of the District to find ourselves at Sequoia in Georgetown, near Duncan's new apartment. He used to live in Navy Yard, close to where we cleaned up this morning, but sublets the apartment to Charlotte and Hayden now. Something about not wanting to live in your little brother's sex den, which fair.

"Well, I don't know about anyone else, but I'm getting a mimosa," Hayden announced, Hunter quickly following behind. I scanned the drinks menu, not interested in that much sugar or carbonation right now.

"Want to do the scotch tasting they have?" Duncan asked from my left side. "I'm buying."

I shrugged. "Sounds good to me. And of course you are. I don't know that any of us have paid for a meal we've eaten with you in the last five years."

Duncan didn't even have the good graces to look ashamed. Old habits died hard, and providing for his brothers was one of the longest-lasting inclinations for my older brother.

We put in our drink orders with Eduardo, our server. Duncan and I sat facing the Potomac, the sun shining on our faces, taking full advantage of the outdoor seating the restaurant boasted. There weren't many boats out given the early spring season, but I wondered if we might see the crew team from the university row by. I shuddered, not envying their all-weather training regimen.

"So guys, what's new?" I asked, ending the lull in conversation as Hayden put down his menu, the last of our group to do so.

"That's rich coming from the guy who told us about his engagement in a text message," Hunter snarked.

"Hey now, some of us found out by seeing her in the flesh and having Preston's boss break the news," Hayden added.

"Can I at least get a drink before we start in on this?" I groaned, very glad Jax accepted Laurel's invitation for brunch, so she wasn't faced with this interrogation. Like magic, Eduardo and a colleague appeared, setting our drinks down with a flourish.

"To pulling teeth," Duncan toasted, and even I laughed good-naturedly as our glasses clinked together in the center of the table. We all took a sip before Eduardo returned to take our orders.

It seemed all my excuses had run out, so I steeled myself and looked at each of my brothers in turn. "All right, let's have it."

Duncan turned to me and started. "You have to understand why we're concerned. We didn't even know you were dating someone and then you show up at a work event and you're engaged? It seems an awful lot like your relationship with Diana."

I swallowed another sip of my scotch, understanding where he was coming from. "Yeah, well, I never proposed to Diana, did I?"

"Thank fuck for that," Hunter said. Hayden smacked him upside the head, but added, "He's not wrong, though."

"Diana just wanted to be a politician's wife. She thought it would be all glamour and parties and inside favors. She didn't care about me or the issues I cared about. Jax isn't like that."

"You see that now," Hayden said seriously. "But you were blinded by love, lust, beauty, and whatever it was that made you turn a blind eye to Diana's true nature. If Duncan hadn't uncovered her plan to announce you were running for the House . . ."

I grimaced. My intentions to get a job and work for a congressperson before running for office hadn't sat well with Diana. She thought if she leaked to the press my plans to run, I'd have to go through with it, and would need her by my side as the doting partner.

"Okay, yes, my judge of character may not have been the best. But I'm older and wiser now," I protested.

"You also haven't dated anyone at all since then," Duncan said, raising his eyebrow.

"That's also true, but that's because I've been so wary. Doesn't the fact that I let Jax in count for anything?" I realized I was arguing about a fake relationship, but the truth in my words struck me. From the moment I rescued Jax on the visitors center floor, something drew me to her. I couldn't tell her no when she asked me to dinner, and I hadn't wanted to tell her no when she presented me with her plan. Something about her seeped through my barriers and made me want to let her into my life, even in this unconventional way.

"I suppose it does," Duncan said, as if he were weighing my words. "Does she know you're planning to run for office?"

"She does." I hesitated, and decided now was a better time to deliver my news than through another group text later this year. "I'm going to announce my candidacy for the House after the Senate election this year. I'm running in the next cycle."

Cheers and congratulations erupted from the table, and my brother signaled Eduardo for another glass of scotch for all of us. Something much more expensive and worthy of a celebration than what was included in our flight. Only after we had toasted the good news, and our food had arrived, did Duncan bring the conversation back around.

"So I have to ask, did you make the decision about the timing to run before or after you proposed?"

I thought about how to answer that question, not wanting to build in any more lies. "I decided before I proposed, but Jax knew I had been thinking about it. She actually called me out on the timing before I could tell her my final decision."

I held up my hand as Duncan started to interrupt. "But I promise it's different. Jax cares about people and issues like I do. She left a political reporting job to come work for the senator's office because she saw how overworked and stressed I had become." That was mostly true.

"I understand it seems fast and sudden, but you said it yourself, Dunc. She shows up. She's been showing up for me and I have faith she'll keep showing up." I said this with conviction because I knew it to be true. Even when she was mad at me over the couch, she still came to the interview instead of blowing me off and finding another job on her own. "Can you please just trust me and move on?"

I looked at each brother, waiting for them to nod. I knew their concern came from a place of love, and I hated lying to them. I needed this conversation to be over.

"All right, deal. But I would like to have more family dinners when our schedules line up. Whoever happens to be in town. If she's going to be around, I want to get to know her better."

I swallowed another mouthful of scotch, the burning of it down my throat matching the burning of my conscience. What would happen when Jax and I eventually went our separate ways? We may well extend our arrangement past the initial three months, but eventually one of us would want out. At the very least, in our current circumstances, it meant a sexless existence. That had been my reality for the last several years, but I doubted the same rang true for her.

"You got it," I responded, hoping the smile on my face looked natural and not forced.

"So Hunter," Duncan turned on the youngest Brandt brother present. "What's new with you?"

"And here I thought you'd never ask," he drawled, a knowing smirk on his face. His expression turned serious as he looked at his twin, who nodded encouragingly. "Actually, I do have some news. I'm about six weeks away from finishing my culinary certification at the community college in Winterberry Glen."

I put my hand on Duncan's arm before he could signal for another round of scotch. We needed to be able to walk out of this place. "That's so great, Hunter. I had no idea you liked to cook."

He laughed. "Honestly, neither did I. But after I moved out of Dad's and Margaret's a few years ago, way later than I should have," he added wryly. "I got sick of eating take out. I started out small and worked my way up to recipes I found online.

"I've made a few things for dinners at Dad's place, but it's sort of sad to not have anyone to cook for. So, I found this program and Hayden helped me with the tuition, so I didn't have to tell anyone. I know I have a habit of starting things and not finishing them. Part of me wanted to wait until I finished to tell anyone, but then I realized I had to sit through all of your graduations, so maybe it was time you returned the favor."

"Absolutely," I said, and Duncan echoed me. "Tell us the date and we'll be there."

Hunter looked bashful. "The program is finished in April, but I walk in May. I'll get you all the info so you can mark it in your calendars."

Duncan and I made eye contact, and I nodded. "I think it's time for that extra round of scotch after all."

We sat at the table, much longer than we deserved, Duncan slipping Eduardo a few hundreds from his billfold to make up for the lost turnover. It had been months since we all were able to spend time together, and even longer since it was a casual afternoon without any agenda or time constraints. We even Face-Timed Spencer for a few minutes, before dirty looks from our neighbors made us promise to call him back individually over the next few days.

Eventually, Duncan pushed back from the table, announcing he had some work that needed attending to at the office.

"Is work code for something else?" Hunter asked. Duncan gave him a sly smile, and hugged us each in turn, turning toward the exit with a salute.

"I wonder if Charlotte is up for a mid-afternoon *work* session," Hayden mused, checking his phone. I shuddered. I knew all my brothers weren't hard up for sex, but I didn't need the fact shoved right in my face.

"What about Hunter? He's staying with you guys, right?"

"He has that friend from his job at the auto body shop who lives here now he's going to meet for a drink, right, Hunt?"

"Right," Hunter answered, checking his phone and not meeting either of our eyes. Only the fact that mixing champagne and scotch did not make a good combination for Hayden did his twin sense not pick up that Hunter was obviously lying.

"She says if I come home right now, she'll let us play secretary/boss," Hayden said, pushing his chair back so fast it scraped on the floor, "so I'm out." He saluted us and left the room as fast as polite company would allow.

"I'm positive she did not want him to tell us that," Hunter said, watching his twin's departing figure.

"He'll be okay to get home, right?" I wondered if I should follow him.

"Oh yeah. Charlotte's like a homing signal for him. He won't let her down," he answered. Looking at his phone again, a small smile appeared.

"So, who are you really meeting?" I asked, nodding at the phone he tried to put casually face down on the table. Hunter considered me for a moment. "I'm your big brother. I'm allowed to worry," I said, quoting Duncan. "I know you can take care of yourself, but if you're meeting someone different from who you're leading Hayden to believe . . ."

"It's just this girl I met on Tinder. She likes that I'm only in town for the weekend, and I believe her when she says she doesn't normally do the random thing. And she just told me . . . well, she seems really excited to meet up. I don't have her name, but her username is WeatherGirl85."

"Well, you know, just use protection, keep your location on, all that." Hunter rolled his eyes at me. "God, do I sound like Duncan right now?" He laughed, while nodding. "Let's get out of here before I tell you to open a Roth IRA or something." We both stood and hugged before walking toward the exit.

"I'm going to hit the head before I leave. It was really good to see you, Hunter. And I'm proud of you."

"Thanks, Prez," he said. "That means a lot."

"Now, get out of here, go get some," I said, cringing as I heard myself and turning around before I could become even more of a cliché.

"You too, bro." I heard Hunter call as I entered the men's room. I stopped at the sink and looked at myself in the mirror. The only place I wanted to get some from right now was closed for business. Because in my slightly tipsy state, as I was alone in this fancy-as-fuck restroom, I could admit it. I wanted my fake fiancée. And I had no idea what to do about it.

CHAPTER
Sixteen

JAX

Laurel indeed knew just the place, and all four of us dropped a good chunk of change in the little boutique she took us to that afternoon. Laurel and Caitlin kept their purchases a secret from each other. Michelle bought something for her meet up that night, which was definitely on. We all made plans to get drinks next week to hear all about it. Michelle's night that was. Laurel would tell me at the office without much prompting, if I let her.

Now back at Preston's apartment, the mimosas had practically worn off, and I was getting cold feet. I decided to try on what I bought again, the last item being a royal blue lace and silk nightie. The mirror in the bathroom cut me off at the waist, and I couldn't get a full body view without contorting myself into a weird position. Not exactly the sexy image I wanted to portray. I checked my phone, and seeing nothing from Preston, decided to risk using the full-length mirror inside the coat closet in the entryway.

I opened the closet door and stepped back. Blue happened to be my favorite color because, yes, it did bring out my eyes. The fact that Preston had noticed made it a bonus. The lace on the cups was a floral pattern, allowing just a glimpse of pink to show through. The long silk layers that started at the top of my rib cage flowed to just below my ass. Those pieces parted just above my navel if you pulled them in opposite directions, but fell almost demurely the way they hung right now.

"Okay, it's a good look," I muttered, my hands on my hips. "But what am I doing? We're adults. Surely we can talk about this."

Suddenly, a key sounded in the lock and a second later the outside door bounced off the closet door, rebounding back with a thwack.

"Ouch. Fuck!" It seemed that thwack was the door making contact with the person trying to enter.

"Shit, Preston, I'm sorry." I shut the closet door, opened the front door, and pulled him inside. "Are you okay? Let me see." I pulled his hand off his forehead where he was rubbing it, and saw a red welt forming. "I can't see in this dim light. Come into the living room. Do you need some ice?"

I pushed the front door shut and dragged Preston into the living room where there was more light. It was then I noticed his eyes were zeroed in on my chest and I remembered what I was doing when he came in.

"What . . . what are you wearing?" Preston asked, his eyes tracing me from the hem of the skirt, up to one of the straps that had now fallen off my shoulder and onto my arm.

"Oh, this old thing?" I asked fixing my strap, trying to play it off. It didn't work.

"We did some shopping after brunch and I was just, trying things on, to see if I wanted to take them back or not. A bit of buyer's remorse, you know. Let me grab my robe, and then I'll get you some ice."

Preston grabbed my arm, stopping my motion and my rambling. "If you're uncomfortable, by all means, cover up. But you don't need to do so on my account. You look beautiful. I . . . I think it's a keeper."

My skin warmed from my cheeks through my chest at his

praise. His eyes were on mine now, showing me the sincerity behind his words. It seemed I didn't have to worry about seducing Preston. This was a man ready to be seduced.

I lightly pulled out of his grasp. "I'd feel a lot better about accepting that compliment if I knew for sure you weren't concussed." I grabbed my robe from the back of the bathroom door, tying the sash. "Sit down. I'm going to get you that ice."

Preston sat, but his eyes burned, focused on my every move while I grabbed ice from the freezer, wrapped it in a towel, and brought it over to him.

"Here," I said, offering him the bag of ice with one hand. Preston grabbed that hand, and pulled toward him, causing me to land on his lap. He arranged me so I straddled his legs, my face just above his.

"Here," he echoed. "This way you can hold the ice on my forehead, and check out my pupils, or whatever other concussion tests you have in mind. But I promise, I'm fine."

I licked my lips nervously, his eyes following the movement. His pupils did seem to be a normal size.

"What day is it?" I asked.

"It's Saturday."

"How many brothers do you have?"

"Too many." I glared at him. "Four."

"And how many are in town right now?"

"Three."

I lifted the ice off his forehead. The swelling had already gone down from the cold.

"I guess it just sounded a lot worse than it actually was."

Preston nodded. "I honestly think it hit my foot and my head at the same time. My toe got the brunt of it."

"Do you need me to check that too?" I asked, half ready to get on the floor if he asked me to.

"I'd rather you told me why you went lingerie shopping today, buying something in my favorite color on you." He stared at my robe like it offended him, hiding the blue silk from his eyes.

"Do I have to be sitting on your lap for that?"

Preston withdrew his hands from my hips and leaned back into the cushion giving me as much space as he could, considering I was on top of him. I regretted the question immediately. "Of course not. You never have to do anything you don't want to do with me."

Something further thawed in my chest. This man could be my undoing, if I let him. Maybe even if I didn't.

"I mean, you are pretty comfortable." I shifted slightly, discovering a hard bulge in Preston's pants. I raised an eyebrow, and he retracted further into the couch.

"Sorry, sorry. I mean, I'm not sorry. You're gorgeous and you're sitting on me, and I'm only human. But I am sorry it reared its head while we're trying to have a conversation."

I couldn't help my giggle. "Reared its head?"

Preston shrugged, a big smile on his face. "So, Jax. Why did you go lingerie shopping?"

"I thought I might try to seduce you," I said, meeting his gaze.

"And what happened to not playing with fire and keeping physical touches to necessity only?"

I shrugged, trying to play it cool, though my heart was beating wildly. "I suppose I've had a change of heart."

"Any particular reason?"

"Does it matter if there was?" I responded, my reflex to keep some cards close to my chest winning out.

Something flickered across Preston's face. "I suppose it doesn't."

Part of me wanted to follow that flicker, but I worried that path led to the undoing I was so desperate to avoid. Best to keep things simple and straightforward.

"Okay. Well." I untied the knot holding my robe together. Preston sat up straight, his eyes following my movements. "I think we should have some ground rules."

Preston's throat bobbed as he swallowed. "Ground rules," he repeated.

"Just to try and avoid getting burned by that fire." I slid the robe off my shoulders. Apparently, a little seduction was still in bounds after all.

"I'm listening," Preston said, his eyes roving over the reemerged blue fabric.

Before I could list any rules, Preston's phone rang, the vibrations resounding against my thigh. His head thunked to my collarbone.

"That's the senator's ringtone."

"Okay, well put your phone on Do Not Disturb." The phone stopped ringing while I spoke. "Oh, never mind. Now where were we?"

The phone started ringing again.

"My phone's been on Do Not Disturb all day," Preston picked up his head to look at me. "He won't stop until I pick up."

I slid off his lap and onto the couch next to him, so he could get to his phone in his pocket. "The senator is an exception for your Do Not Disturb?"

"Can we not discuss work/life boundaries right now?" Preston adjusted himself as he picked up.

"Hell—"

I heard the senator cut off his greeting, speaking quickly into the phone. Preston's eyes widened as he listened.

"Yes, she's here." His eyes cut my way as he listened more. "Understood. We'll be there in an hour."

He hung up and immediately started typing furiously on his phone.

"Where are we going?" I said, tying my robe again. The moment had passed. Again. Frustration at being cock blocked by our boss on a day off was only held back by interest in the vigor with which Preston typed. Something big happened.

"A school board is calling a last-minute vote on reversing their gender bathroom policy on Monday night. The parents of the teenager at the center of the storm got ahold of Senator Marsden somehow and want him to be at the meeting. With the primary less than two weeks away, he can't say no, and he wants us both there. He flew out earlier today. He wants us on the 8:30 flight out of DCA."

I stood up, a fire burning in my chest that had nothing to do with how close my body had been to Preston's moments earlier. He cared about the work the senator did, the work he hoped to do some day, so much. It was hard not to feel inspired.

"All right then, I guess we better pack." I walked over to the coat closet to grab our suitcases. I put them in the middle of the living room and then decided to get dressed before I did any more prep.

"Hey, Jax?" Preston called, prompting me to turn around at the doorway to the bathroom, his back to me as he stacked clothes in his suitcase on top of the dresser.

"Yeah?"

"Make sure you pack that nightie, okay? And bring those ground rules of yours. We'll have to hammer them out on the plane. The senator's only getting us one room, and I sure as hell hope there's only one bed."

I melted slightly against the doorframe, glad he couldn't see me, before turning back and closing myself off from Preston and his swoony ideas. The fire from before returned, merging with the admiration I felt for Preston and his commitment to his beliefs. Maybe the moment hadn't passed after all.

CHAPTER
Seventeen

PRESTON

Being this horny on a plane was a new experience for me. Thankfully, the only two seats left on the flight were first class, which gave perks of extra leg room and assured us our own row. Every step of the boarding process seemed to take twice as long, now that the motivation to make it through the short flight and whatever work session Mitchell had waiting for us sat beside me, smelling like a damn dream. I ached to get her alone again.

"So," Jax said, turning to face me, her back against the window in the dim airplane light.

"So," I responded, my eyes searching out the features of her face, eyes adjusting to the darkness.

"You wanted my ground rules. Do you have any of your own?" she asked, sipping the Diet Coke the flight attendant brought her after we reached cruising altitude.

"I might. Let's hear yours first."

Jax looked like she wanted to argue. "Okay. First, we keep the three-month trial end date. Getting more physical doesn't change that."

I nodded, urging her to continue.

"This doesn't change what we are to each other. If someone starts to feel feelings, they say so and everything stops."

I swallowed, reaching for my own glass of water. I had no experience separating sex from emotions. But I knew I wanted Jax, so if that's what it took to have her, I'd agree.

"Agreed. Anything else?" I asked

"Foreplay goes both ways."

I choked on my water. "Obviously," I said.

"And communication is key. If you don't like something, if someone isn't in the mood or isn't feeling up to it, speak up and no guilting anyone into anything."

A look of horror had to be on my face, I was sure of it. "I would hope that's a given. I can't decide if I never want to know why you had to say that, or if I should go punch some guy's face in."

Jax shrugged. "Girls too. But when you have an invisible illness, sometimes people don't always believe you when you speak up."

I put my hand on her arm. "I told you before, you never have to do anything with me you don't want to do. You're safe with me."

Jax looked me in the eye for a moment before answering. "I know I am." She cleared her throat. "So, anything you want to add?"

"It might slot under that communication, but don't lie to me. If you aren't, um, *getting there*, help me help you. Don't fake it. Okay?" I felt torn open, a part of my relationship with Diana my brothers didn't even know about.

Jax studied me. "Now I feel the need to go punch some faces in."

I laughed without humor. "It's not worth it. But yeah. That's my ground rule."

"Shake on it?" Jax held her hand out toward mine. I took it, shaking once, before twisting our arms so her hand was on top. I brought it to my mouth, dropping a featherlight kiss on each of her knuckles, before turning her hand over, laying a kiss on her open palm and setting her hand on my leg. I rested mine on top, keeping hers there.

"You know." Jax let out a shaky breath. "I think we're going to be just fine. You seem to have a direct line to my groin with your mouth."

I closed my eyes at her words, feeling my own groin tightening. This type of flight was not one to pass out pillows and blankets, so I needed to keep myself under control. Jax opening and closing her fingers where they rested on my leg did not help matters.

"The senator's going to want to go right into a strategy session when we land," I said, keeping my eyes closed.

Jax let out a sigh. "I figured. Well, anticipation makes the payoff all that much sweeter." She removed her hand from mine, tucking herself into a ball against the window. "Wake me when we land."

I knew I should try to catch a few minutes of shut eye too, considering it could be a late night with Senator Marsden and then hopefully a *late* night with Jax. I was too keyed up though. Instead, my mind raced between what we were flying here to do and what I wanted to do to the woman sitting next to me.

The strategy session Senator Marsden dragged us to after we landed lasted until 2:00 a.m. He finally set us free with a parting shout to meet him for breakfast at the hotel restaurant at 8:00 a.m. sharp.

Jax and I walked side by side from the elevator to our hotel room. Waves of exhaustion radiated off her and I certainly fared no better. Each of my feet seemed to weigh fifty pounds on their own and the hallway looked never ending.

"Here we are." Jax pointed to room 829. Hotel staff had brought our luggage up when we arrived, so we hadn't seen the room yet. I held the key card against the sensor and pushed the door open when the light turned green. A standard mid-tier hotel room lay before us, with a bathroom to the right, a coffee bar and mini fridge to the left, and yes, only one king-sized bed in the center of the room.

"No couch for you to escape to," Jax joked as she plopped onto the bed, spread out like a starfish. "On an unrelated note, I'm not sure I've ever been this tired in my life."

I nudged her foot with mine. "Get up and wash your face. You'll be happy you did in the morning."

Jax leaned up on her elbows, studying me. "I will feel better in the morning with a clean face. But don't you want to, you know . . ."

I leaned over the top of her, my hand on the mattress next to her head with my arm fully extended, very careful to be sure no part of my body brushed hers. "Adhering to rule number four, I want to crawl into this bed with you, pull you against my body" —I heard her intake a breath—"and sleep."

Jax smacked my forearm as I laughed, straightening so I stood upright again.

"You're probably right." She rubbed her hands over her face. "Do you want the bathroom first?"

"No, you go right ahead."

She heaved herself off the bed, making her way to her bag on a luggage stand. After she gathered what she needed, she walked to the bathroom, shooting me a smile over her shoulder before closing the door behind her.

I walked over to the sliding glass door and looked out into the dark night, overlooking the parking lot of the hotel. As amped up as I had been before, I didn't want the first time Jax and I were together to be like this. Exhausted, dirty, and maybe a little hungover from brunch over twelve hours ago. At the risk of getting my emotions involved, I knew Jax was special and deserved more than that.

Seeing movement reflected in the glass from the room behind me, I turned around to see Jax sliding into bed.

"Bathroom's all yours," she said, plugging her phone in on the side table and propping herself up slightly on the pillows. I stopped by my bag and got myself ready for bed, returning from the bathroom to see Jax in the same position, with a concerned look on her face.

"Everything okay?" I asked.

"Huh?" She met my eyes. "Oh yes, fine. I've been told before I have a 'concerned reading face' that doesn't necessarily match what I'm reading. In fact, a dragon and human woman are about to get it on."

"Perhaps some concern is warranted though. Assuming the dragon is male, I could imagine some fit issues," I said, folding the covers back on my side and sliding into bed next to her. I laid on my side, propping my head on my hand.

"Ah, but in this world, they have a magical salve to soothe any soreness created by a size mismatch. All bases are covered." Jax matched my position, setting her phone down.

"You know, I've never read a romance novel. You seem to like them a lot."

Averting her eyes, Jax said, "You could say that. They're a big part of my life."

"Maybe you could recommend one for me to read sometime," I said, finding I meant it. "Maybe no dragons for my first go, though."

"I could probably find something you like."

I sat up and pulled my T-shirt over my head, leaving me in my flannel pajama pants. Jax's eyes lingered on my chest as I settled on my back.

"What?" I asked. "I noticed you didn't have any bottoms on. I thought I'd even us out and sleep without a top on. Honestly, sleeping in a shirt for the past few weeks has been killing me."

"Same with me and pants," Jax confessed. "I slipped them off every night after the lights went out."

"Smart woman." I reached over and tucked some hair that had come out of Jax's ponytail behind her ear. "Speaking of lights out, it's probably past time to get some sleep."

"I got it," Jax said, twisting toward the lamp to turn it off, her shirt stretching against her breasts, giving me a hint she wasn't wearing a bra either. "Last chance for a pillow boundary for your virtue," she said as she settled down next to me.

"I think I'll risk it," I said, rolling over, so I could sling my arm across her waist and nuzzle my face in her hair, breathing deeply. My eyes grew heavy as I felt her warmth against me and inhaled her lavender lotion, this time feeling the silky softness of her skin against mine.

"Goodnight," she whispered into the darkness, her fingers tangling with mine where they rested at her side.

"Night," I muttered into her neck. As the world faded away, the knowledge I was falling right to sleep on a first night away from home dawned on me, but the thought disappeared in the next instant as sleep engulfed me.

We woke up much as we had those first mornings in my apartment, limbs tangled, Jax's back to my chest. The knowledge that we both wanted to be here, touching, made all the difference. I picked my head up to spy the time on the bedside clock. Early morning light filtered into the room from where we had forgotten to draw the curtain. I knew we needed to get up and start our day, but found it hard to move from this bed.

Though I tried to keep my movements subtle, I felt Jax stir. "Mmm, whattimesit?" she asked, her voice muffled and heavy with sleep.

"A little after 6:30," I answered. "I can get the first shower if you want to sleep a bit longer."

Jax arched her ass back to meet my morning wood, letting

out a sound of appreciation as I did my best to stay still and let her explore.

"We could shower together," she suggested, sounding much more awake.

"What? Together? Now? But . . ." I spluttered.

Jax laughed gently and rolled over to look at me. "Okay, so no morning sex yet. We'll work up to that." She brushed her hand on my cheek, feeling the stubble there. Before I could react to her brief touch, she rolled herself into a sitting position, and stretched, her shirt riding up to reveal pink lace panties. "I'll shower first," she said as I flopped over onto my back, throwing my arm over my eyes.

I peeked as she walked past the bed and found her smirking. She knew exactly what she was doing. I'm not sure I could match her energy, but two could play that game. It's on.

I was right, Jax's game of seduction exceeded my own. How the senator didn't fire us, I'll never be sure. She leaned into my space more than necessary, distracting me with her scent and the feel of her skin on mine. I asked my boss to repeat himself more today than I think I have in the last five years.

He set us free right before dinner, telling us he had a dinner date and he supposed the least he could do after disrupting our weekend was set us free to do the same. I looked at Senator Marsden like he had two heads, which he didn't appreciate, telling me he was happy to demand speech drafts for next week's budget session by tomorrow morning if I'd rather do that. I schooled my face better after that.

"So," I said, once we were alone in the elevator, headed to our room. "Dinner? Or . . .?"

Jax was across the elevator car in a flash, pulling my head down for a kiss. The door opened with a ding and had me pulling back in a daze.

"Sorry," she said, biting her lip, looking anything but. "I've wanted to do that all day, especially after you took my teasing so well."

A shudder racked my body at her words, a current of warmth trailing down my spine.

"Interesting," Jax appraised me with curious eyes. "Preston, do you . . ." she trailed off, biting her lip as we passed a family with children in the hallway. We walked in silence until we got to the room, me eyeing her curiously.

"Do I what?" I asked, as soon as the door closed behind us.

"Do you like being praised in the bedroom?" I looked at her, feeling confused. She must have picked up on this, as she kept going. "What I mean is, do you like being told when you do something well? Being told you're good at something, that you're simply good?"

My cheeks got warm as I realized our rules meant I had to be honest in this moment. "I . . . I don't know." Jax kept quiet, waiting for me to continue. "My ex, you know, she wasn't honest with me about my, well, my performance."

Jax waved her hand, as if wanting to wave away the bad juju of Diana. "Okay, well, what about other women you've been with?"

I sucked in a deep breath. "I haven't been with anyone else," I said, having trouble meeting Jax's eyes.

"Oh, Brandt," she said, her voice compelling me to look up. "Are you sure you want to do this?"

CHAPTER
Eighteen

I held my breath, waiting for Preston's answer. I'd never have proposed a friends-with-benefits scenario if I knew he had only been with one woman. I wanted to wring that bitty's neck earlier when I thought she simply dented his confidence, but now that I knew she comprised his only frame of reference? I'm not sure this was a good idea anymore.

"Yes," Preston exhaled, his sincerity apparent in his open body language.

"You're sure? We can go back to pillow walls, or see if we can get a different room with two beds or a couch. I can't offer you the real deal, Preston. This is two consenting adults having sex because they're in a situation I previously thought only existed in books."

Preston nodded. "I know. Part of the reason there's only been Diana is because I'm so focused on my goals, on running for Congress. I don't want anything more. It only distracted me before."

Even though I set the boundary, I said it first, hearing Preston tell me he didn't want more created an ache in my chest. I shook myself, moving past it. Remnants of feeling like I'd always be alone. I was better off on my own, but a girl had to eat, and Preston was, apparently, ready and willing.

"All right then, if you're sure."

"I'm sure," Preston's voice wavered. "But I'm not convinced how good it'll be." I raised my eyebrow. "I mean, I know it's going to be great for me. But if she had to fake it all the time, that must mean . . ."

I held up a hand to cut him off. "That doesn't mean anything. Maybe she didn't know her own body well enough to guide you or didn't trust you enough to be vulnerable. Or some other explanation that you should not hold on to as your fault. I told you I feel safe with you. Do you feel safe with me?"

He nodded, his eyes wide.

"Then we'll be just fine."

Preston closed his eyes for a moment, took a deep breath, and nodded again. He took a step toward me, one hand in my hair and one on my waist. And then Preston Brandt kissed me— he kissed me like he meant it.

It was the type of kiss that knew it was leading to more. His lips moved like he had something to prove, like he was ready to give me his all. I answered in kind, trying to tell him he could take the lead, I would follow him.

Preston pushed me back toward the bed as his tongue traced the seam of my mouth, asking for entry. I opened, and the kiss deepened, no longer sending a message of anything except "I want you, I want this." That was okay by me.

The back of my legs hit the bed, and we fell back in a heap. My fingers were tangled in Preston's hair as he peppered kisses down my neck, pulling at the top of my button-down shirt to get at my collarbone.

"You know, business attire is hot, but really restrictive," I said, moaning the last word as Preston found a sensitive spot where my neck met my shoulder. Would he make it a point to search for more? Shuddering against him, I hoped so.

He chuckled against my skin, shrugging out of his jacket and throwing it across the room before returning to his path, tracing up to my other ear. "Yeah, in the movies there are always a lot more flying clothes."

"We got a bit distracted by all that talking," I said, working his tie loose and untucking his shirt. Preston pulled back a bit before I realized my mistake. "Very necessary talking. Anything else would have been jumping the gun." I started at the bottom of his shirt, taking one button at a time.

"You know, in the movies there's a lot more shirt ripping and buttons flying too," he said, as I slid one shoulder down, and then the other. He kneeled upright to finish taking it off himself.

"It's true, but I love that shirt on you. It's one of my favorites. And honestly, the ripping is harder than it looks," I said, starting to unbutton my own shirt.

"Wait," Preston said, stopping my hands immediately. "I want to do that." His eyes had darkened to a color I had never seen on him before. He reached down to take over where my fingers left off.

The heat of his gaze seared each inch of skin he exposed. The intensity in his eyes felt like he wanted to remember every single frame of this moment. He leaned down to kiss the exposed skin, pulling down one bra cup, and then the other. Moving to my nipple, he took it in his mouth, licking tentatively while his hand worked my other breast.

"You can be rougher than that," I said, arching into his touch. "Yesss," I hissed as he bit down gently, licking to soothe the sting before sucking with more pressure than before. "That's so good." He hummed against my skin, moving his mouth over to repeat the actions on the other side, while tracing a hand down my ribcage to my hip bone.

His eyes met mine, almost as if looking for direction. I wanted to give him permission to take whatever he wanted.

"What do you want to do now?" I asked, running a hand through his hair and tugging on the strands a bit.

"I . . . I'd like to taste you." His face set with determination, yet still asking permission. I nodded, finding it hard to speak.

I'd never thought of the removal of tights as particularly erotic, but having a man as handsome and attentive as Preston following the path of skin revealed from my inner thighs to the top of my feet changed things. I lay on the bed, chest heaving. My boobs trussed up above my bra cups, only panties remaining between me and the warm exhales of breath on my core. Preston's hands shook slightly as he reached for the waistband of my underwear, breathing in a steadying breath, and he peeled them down. I lifted my hips to help him.

He lay with his chest flat on the bed, ass propped in the air, making me wish I could reach and give it a squeeze. I lost that train of thought as Preston bent one of my legs, and then the other, baring me to him. He ran a finger through my wetness, causing my hips to follow his path, seeking more. His eyes met mine, seeking approval, guidance, something.

"You've got great instincts, baby. Follow them."

He leaned his head down, taking a slow, tentative lick up my core to my clit. I shivered at the contact, but needed more.

"A little firmer, a little faster. I promise you won't drown," I said, propping up on my elbows so I could take in the sight of him between my legs.

He lapped his tongue a few more times, circling my clit. "I dunno. If I had to drown somewhere, I think this might be my choice." The warm puffs of air from his words tickled, making me desperate for more pressure.

"With respect," I gritted out. "Less talking, more licking, fingering, *something*." I fisted the blankets to stop from spreading myself open. I wanted to come, but I wanted Preston to gain his confidence even more. Was that growth?

Preston dove back in, spearing me with his tongue, before focusing his attention on my clit. He inserted one finger, and then two, working them in and out of my core. The flat of his tongue stroked up my clit, alternating with a strong suction.

"Right there. Just that pressure on my clit. That's so good." My arms shook, then gave out, my back hitting the mattress, but only the nerve endings between my thighs were transmitting sensation. What he lacked in experienced skill, he made up for in enthusiasm and ability to follow direction.

I felt the bed moving by my feet and lifted my head to see Preston humping the bed beneath him, seeking friction of his own. I lifted a foot and put it on his back, pinning his hips against the bed. He pulled his mouth away from me, his fingers still moving inside me slowly, my wetness shiny around his lips.

"I have plans for this later. If you'd keep still." He stopped fighting to push against my foot immediately and put his mouth back on my clit, redoubling his efforts. "That's a good boy," I said, no longer consciously seeking opportunities to praise Preston, the words just slipped out. He groaned into me, the vibrations pushing me toward the top of the peak just before the long fall.

"Yes, I'm almost there. Keep going." And he did until my muscles seized and my mouth opened in a silent scream. Preston's mouth pressed kisses against the inside of my leg, while his fingers continued to move, carrying me through the last waves of my orgasm. Finally opening my eyes, I smiled, the curve growing as his grin answered me.

"C'mon up here," I said, pawing at his shoulder. He wiped his face against my leg before crawling up, trailing kisses until his mouth met mine. I grabbed his head on both sides, keeping his lips pressed on mine, tasting myself on his kiss.

Our kiss slowed until he pulled back. "Hi," he said, almost shyly.

"Hi yourself," I said, running my fingers through his hair. If Preston was capable of purring, I think brushing his hair like this would do it.

"So, you mentioned plans," Preston said, pushing his hips gently into my leg, reminding me how incredibly hard he still was.

"I'd love to have you inside me," I said. "In my mouth or my pussy. It's your choice. There's no pressure. You can also just jack off on my tits if you want."

Preston's jaw dropped slightly. "Are you sure you're real and laying here?"

I laughed. "I've done a lot of communicating about sex." At Preston's raised eyebrow, I smacked his shoulder. I caught him off guard and used that to my advantage to flip him.

"I will not be slut shamed, but that's also not what I mean." Writing sex scenes for a living made it easier, at least for me, to say what I wanted out loud. Wanting to distract Preston before he could ask any more questions, I unclasped my bra, sliding it down my arms. I took my turn trailing kisses down his neck. I bit down on his nipple, soothing the sting when he gasped out loud and thrust his hips up into mine.

"So responsive. Such a good boy," I said, gripping his cock through the fabric. Preston moaned out loud, grinding against my palm. Wanting to free him from his pants prison, I undid his belt and opened his fly. A damp spot decorated the front of his navy boxer briefs. As I pulled the waistband down, his cock sprung free. I stroked him, up and down, twisting my hand over the tip. I intentionally used light pressure, wanting to work him into a bit of a frenzy.

"You're killing me down there," Preston said, tipping his chin into his chest to meet my eyes.

"You're not telling me what you want," I said, squeezing tighter for one pass of his cock, smirking at the answering thrust, before loosening my grip again.

"I'd very much like it if you rode me now." He gasped.

"I'd like that too. Be right back." I got up to grab a condom out of my bag. The intensity of Preston's gaze on my ass was palpable as I opened the pocket. Without turning around, I detected the rustle of his pants coming the rest of the way off. I grabbed a strip of three condoms out of my bag, just in case.

Turning my attention toward the bed, I saw Preston slightly

propped up on pillows, his hand moving up and down his cock. I licked my lips, dying for a taste of my own. Climbing back on the bed, I said, "Now isn't that a picture."

Tearing a condom free from the strip, I opened the foil and took Preston in my mouth, to the back of my throat for one, two strokes. "You're not the only one who wanted a taste."

I straddled his hips, rolling the condom down to his base, before holding him tall. I felt him breach my entrance and inhaled a breath.

"I'm going to need to take this slow," I said through gritted teeth, inching my way onto his thickness.

"The slow torture is worth every second," he said, his hands on my hips, helping to control my descent. One hand on his chest, I reached down and stroked my clit, the extra attention helping me to open and slide down until he was fully inside.

"Good?" he asked.

"Good," I answered. "You?"

"Never better," he answered. His eyes were trained on mine and again displayed his sincerity. He really needed to work on his poker face if he was going to survive in politics.

"Okay. I'm going to move now," I said, pushing up until only the tip remained in my core and sliding back down. The next movement much quicker. We found a rhythm, Preston's hips coming up to meet my down thrusts. My legs started to shake, pitching me forward, so my chest met his.

Preston thrust up into me, finding that spot inside me that made me cry out. "Yes, right there," I heard myself shout as we picked up the pace before he stilled deep inside me, a groan from deep in his chest sounding out.

We lay there for a moment, our breathing heavy, our sweat covered bodies touching. As our breaths normalized, I lifted off him with a slight wince and rolled to the side. I tucked myself into him as he dealt with the condom. Something told me Preston would need the contact. *I certainly wasn't doing it for me*, I told myself.

"Okay, so at the risk of ruining the mood . . . you came when I ate you out, but not just then, right?" Preston said, looking pained.

I put my hand on his chest. "Yes. Penetrative sex isn't the easiest way for me to finish."

He covered his face with the hand not currently wrapped around me. "I wish I would have known that."

I removed his hand and entwined our fingers. "I didn't tell you on purpose. I didn't want you in your head more than you already were." I squeezed his hand so he'd look at me.

"Sex isn't a tit-for-tat endeavor, though if we're keeping track, the score is one-to-one. Helping you reach pleasure turns me on, and makes sure I have a great time. If we keep on doing this, it's always possible we'll get there. But I promise, I'll never make you feel like a failure or lie to you. I'd appreciate it if you made sure my fiancé didn't feel bad about this too."

He smiled. "I'll do my best to pass the message along."

We lay in silence for a while, his hand tracing up and down my naked back.

"You said 'if we do this again,' but I saw you bring over more condoms, so . . ."

"That's up to you, big guy," I said, with a glance at his crotch, currently covered in a sheet.

He smirked. "I'll see what I can do."

"Go get us some waters out of the mini fridge. We'll need to stay hydrated."

Preston climbed out of bed and ambled over to grab the bottles. "I can feel you staring."

"Just returning the favor and enjoying the view. Do they rank the best asses in Congress? Because whoever you hire as your campaign manager should definitely work to get you on that list. I know these things. I work in Comms, after all."

He tossed a bottle of water my way, twisting a cap off his own and downing half of it as he sat back on the bed.

"I'm not sure that's quite how I want to win my votes, but I guess I better use all the *assets* at my disposal."

"Come use those assets over here," I quipped, feeling myself smiling as Preston kissed me. The worries of this man being my ruin still niggled in the back of my mind, but for once, I allowed myself to remain in the moment, happy.

Epistolary Interlude

Breaking News: Rhode Island Senator's speech at school board goes viral. See his frank defense of gender identity.

Who is the writer behind Senator Marsden's fiery speeches? More on Preston Brandt.

JAX

I spilled coffee on your couch sheets.

PRESTON

I'll wash them when I get home.

JAX

I think we should conserve water. Aren't we in a drought?

PRESTON

I'm not sure the mid-Atlantic has droughts in
March.

JAX

Well, still, it's good to preserve the environment
and all that. Won't that be part of your
platform?

PRESTON

I am indeed pro-environmentalism.

JAX

Maybe you should just sleep in the bed when
you get back.

PRESTON

If you wanted to snuggle, you only needed
to ask.

JAX

A certain part of me is very interested in
snuggling a certain part of you.

And I need help with the Times crossword
today. Anything past Tuesday trips me up.

PRESTON

Yes to both.

But on the off chance there is actually coffee
on the sheets, can you pretreat them? I'll wash
them when I get back tonight, but those sheets
are really soft...

JAX

I can wash a set of sheets, Preston. Whether or
not there was actually coffee, I'll never tell.

After Senator Marsden's press conference goes off the rails, Brandt dodges questions about his own political aspirations.

★　　★　　★

JAX

So, that was . . . something.

PRESTON

asdflkjwoihadlj

JAX

I mean, the language was bad, and he probably shouldn't yell. But he mostly stayed on message.

PRESTON

I don't know that calling the Senate majority leader a "fuckwit" and "twat waffle" is ever actually on message.

JAX

How can I help?

PRESTON

Well, I'm sure there will be lots of requests for statements tomorrow. I don't know that getting a start on them tonight is the answer...

JAX

Not what I meant.

PRESTON

??

OH. Oh.

JAX:

Shower blow job? Drown your sorrows while I
sit on your face? Bend me over the bed and
just drill in?

PRESTON

Yes. All of that. Yes. Walking as quickly as I can
with a half-chub.

*Marsden wins primary challenge in a landslide, sets up November
showdown with known foe, Warfield Pippen*

LAUREL

I'm sorry. Does Preston have a hickey that was
NOT there this morning?

JAX

Are you really asking me about hickeys in a
staff meeting?

Also, how are you sure it wasn't there this
morning?

LAUREL

Preston's left ear seemed like a great place to
stare during the staff ethics seminar we had
this morning. You know, the seminar that was
called because that staffer fucked their Grindr
date in the chamber.

JAX

Well, if anyone did get a hickey today, no rules
outlined in that seminar were broken.

LAUREL

And to think, it all started with bottomless mimosas, a blue teddy, and a dream.

Speaking of, happy hour tomorrow? Michelle's still being mum on that one-night stand a few weeks ago. Maybe you can help me badger her for information.

JAX

If she doesn't cancel on you again, sure. She was happy to get falafel with me last week.

LAUREL

Et tu, Brute?

JAX

Maybe being less dramatic will help.

Marsden cuts ribbon at new Independent Bookstore in Providence, Rhode Island. Celebrations included banned books display, drag queen story time, and author signings.

CHARLOTTE

Last week in Rhode Island was so fun! We should try to do weekly double dates.

HAYDEN

Gross, I don't want to see that much of Preston. Jax, you're welcome anytime.

PRESTON

Get back to your research, Hayden.

HAYDEN

I will, thank you! We already have a handful of
companies interested in an audit.

JAX

I heard you talking to some of the business
owners at the opening, right, Hayden?

CHARLOTTE

Yes! My little networker.

HAYDEN

My little bookworm.

PRESTON

Do you have to do that in the group chat?

JAX

C'mon, pookie, I think it's sweet.

HAYDEN

Ha!

JAX

But yes, Charlotte. As long as we're in town,
we'd love to see more of you guys.

*Capital Weather Gang: The cherry blossoms have bloomed and blown
away, but spring is here to stay. The first 80-degree day is in reach this
weekend.*

CHAPTER
Nineteen

Life before Jax seemed hard to remember. I thought my studio would be cramped with another person living there, but she brightened the space with her humor and smile. Plus, she made me actually want to have balance in my work for the first time in, well, ever. Sure, there were still late nights and unexpected hurdles that cropped up, but putting away my laptop to watch TV no longer made me feel guilty. As long as it wasn't for too long, at least.

It was obvious to me I was falling for Jax. Every morning I told myself this would be the night I followed through on rule number two and told Jax my feelings were involved. And then she'd smile my way or touch my hand and I'd think surely one more day won't hurt. We've made it this far.

But there were parts of Jax that still felt out of my reach. Her late-night laptop work habits were back. A privacy film now covered the screen. Jax claimed this was so the light didn't bother me now that we slept in the same bed. It also conveniently kept me from seeing what she worked on. Anytime I asked questions, she got cagey and changed the subject. So I finally stopped asking.

"Okay, I know that I've never been the one to suggest outdoor time before, but I think we *need* to get outside tomorrow," Jax said, looking at her phone. Only the sheet covered her naked body, while I pulled on a pair of boxers to double check the locks and get us both a glass of water.

She looked sleepy and relaxed from the three orgasms I had rung from her body, though none of them on my cock. I knew Jax was getting off, but this barrier between us still bothered me. Maybe it was a good thing, maintaining this one bit of separation. It might be all that stopped me from being completely in love with a woman I could never really have.

"Preston? You okay? Outside time tomorrow?"

I shook myself, tuning back into the moment. "Spending time outside tomorrow sounds great. I was already plotting on how to trick you into agreeing with a plan I have brewing. So, thanks for making it easy."

"I aim to please," she said with an easy grin, leaning up to plant a kiss on my lips before rolling over, punching her pillow into submission to take the shape she liked.

"Time for bed?" I asked, not wanting to draw attention to the fact I noticed she didn't have her computer out.

"Yes, I'm beat. And it sounds like I'll need my strength for secret outdoor surprise day."

"I'm not going to torture you, you know."

"I'll be the judge of that," she answered, her voice muffled by the pillow. "Night, Prez."

The nickname she picked up from spending time with Hayden and Duncan over the past month or so slipped out more and more. While the familiarity it stirred up felt nice, nothing warmed me like the baby or sweetheart that occasionally slipped from her lips. Those instances seemed contained to while we were physical. Just another example of how Jax could compartmentalize when all my lines were blurred and swirled since she'd blown into my life.

Jax turned to face me, her breathing deep and even. The

lights from the street outside let me just make out her features, peaceful and open, while she slept. How I ached for that pure openness while she was awake.

It took a long time before I fell asleep.

My melancholy lasted into the next morning. I tried to hide it from Jax, but as usual, she saw right through me.

"What's up, grumpy Gus? Do you not want to do the outdoor day anymore? We can keep it simple. You don't have to go through with this big plan . . ."

She trailed off, looking uncertain of herself, a look I wasn't used to seeing on her face. Jax hadn't done anything wrong. She continued to play by the rules we set. I was the one having trouble keeping myself in bounds. She didn't deserve that.

"Just need more coffee, I think. C'mon, let's go." I held out my hand, allowing myself to enjoy how her hand felt in mine. I twisted my ring on her finger with my thumb.

"First stop, Eastern Market," I said as we hit the street, walking the few blocks over to the year-round farmer's market. Later in the day, this place would be a zoo, but it was still early enough we could walk the aisles without dodging the crowds.

I steered her into the permanent structure that housed many of the food vendors, especially those that required refrigeration. "We need to pick up from a vendor in here. I have a picnic basket pre-ordered. We worked together to be sure things were low FODMAP and things I knew usually worked for you."

"A picnic?" Jax's face displayed a mixture of emotions. Nervousness, excitement, and disappointment. I understood now the negative came from not being able to simply enjoy something like a picnic without spinning out into digestive worst-case scenarios.

"Trust me? Double check the foods, and then we'll head on to the next stop."

Biting her lip, Jax nodded and followed me to a vendor along the far wall. Telling the employee my name, they handed over an insulated bag for us to inspect. Jax sifted through the contents, a smile breaking on her face as she did.

"Everything in here looks great, Preston. Thank you for thinking of it." She reached up to peck a kiss on my cheek, giving me a matching smile to flash back at her. I paid the employee and thanked them for their help.

"Now, off to find ourselves some bikes," I said, slinging the bag over one arm and holding my other hand out for Jax to grab. If I go down in a pile of flaming heartbreak, it wouldn't be because I didn't go all in on this day.

"Bikes?" Jax asked. "I don't think I've ridden a bicycle in at least a decade."

"Good thing you never forget how," I said, giving her a wink and her hand a squeeze. "Besides, they're electric bikes, so they basically power themselves. You can follow my lead."

"If you say so." She looked skeptical, but her eyes betrayed a hint of excitement.

I stopped next to two rental bikes, one with a platform on the back. I dug the bungee cord the vendor had been kind enough to provide out of the side pocket of the bag and secured our picnic to the back of my bike.

"Ready?" I asked, swinging my leg over the bike. I looked back at Jax expectantly.

"As I'll ever be."

We started our ride through the district, sticking to the bicycle lane on Pennsylvania Avenue as much as possible. The Capitol loomed large in front of us.

"You're not taking me to a picnic on the grounds of the complex where we work, are you?" Jax yelled in order to be heard above the sound of traffic and the distance between us.

"Nope. Onward," I shouted back, turning my head so she could hear me. She'd likely figure out we were headed toward the Mall soon enough, but I'd keep her in suspense a bit longer. The foot traffic increased as we drew even with the Air and Space Museum, the open space filled with locals out for some fresh air and tourists here to visit alike.

As we waited to cross 14th Street, the Washington Monument rose ahead of us with blocks of green space behind. Jax drew even with me. "At least tell me, are we staying in DC or heading the whole way into Virginia?"

"No boundary lines will be crossed, for these plans," I said, cringing internally at my choice of words. I would love it if Jax would cross a boundary or two, but I respected she had her reasons for keeping her emotional distance. "We're almost there."

The light turned green, and we weaved our way past the marble monolith and the World War II Memorial. As we reached the edge of the Reflecting Pool, I spotted a bike stand and steered us in that direction.

"This is close enough," I said, parking my bike and Jax followed suit. I lifted the bag to my shoulder, and before I could start walking, Jax appeared at my side, tangling her hands with mine.

"I sort of liked crossing the city by bike. Taking in all the buildings in a way that's different from driving in a car, but not as slow as walking. I'm not sure I ever would have done it on my own though. Thank you." She squeezed my hand, grasping my forearm with her other hand as we walked the length of pool. Ducks splashed in the pool, freshly descaled from the algae that plagued the still water.

"So, are we visiting Abe?" Jax asked as the marble statue of Lincoln sitting in his chair, looking out across this part of DC, came into view.

"We are," I said. "This is one of my favorite places to people watch or take a break during a long run. You can see so much from up there"—I nodded toward the top of the marble stairs leading to the statue—"but also feel out of the way."

Jax looked around, considering my words.

"Plus," I added, as we started to climb the steps. "There are bathrooms in the visitors center in the basement. Open until 8:oo p.m. tonight."

Her head swung toward me at my words. "I never realized there were bathrooms here. I knew they were scattered along the Mall, but . . . thank you. This is really thoughtful. I can't wait for our picnic."

I ducked my head, my cheeks growing warm. Instead of stepping inside the opening where Abe sat, I guided us to the edge of the elevated platform. People occasionally walked around this corner to take in the view of Arlington National Cemetery across the Potomac, but most people were here for their photo opportunity of the sixteenth president and then they moved on to the next stop on their tour. That left a quiet place to share food and quality time with this woman I was wild about.

I pulled the food from the bag and started laying out the spread between us. Jam and buckwheat biscuits, beef and chicken skewers, grilled with squash and peppers, and a fruit salad of honeydew, cantaloupe, strawberries, and blueberries, plus dairy free pudding for dessert. And finally, I retrieved a bottle of sparkling grape juice from the bag and two plastic cups.

"It's a public park. Actual booze made me nervous," I said when she raised an eyebrow.

"You rule follower," she teased, taking a glass from me. "But also, if you expect me to ride a bicycle back home, it's probably a good idea to not drink and ride. What should we toast to?"

A thousand ideas sped through my mind, but I decided to play it safe.

"To faking it," I said, holding my glass aloft.

Something I couldn't read flickered through Jax's eyes. "To faking it," she echoed, bringing our plastic glasses together with a click.

We picked at our food in relative silence, speaking to point out something or another in the crowd or ask to pass the fruit.

"So," Jax said, pouring herself more juice. "Is this a go-to date suggestion for you when others ask what they should do in the city?"

I shook my head. "No, I don't think I've ever told anyone else how much I love this spot."

"Oh," she said quietly. "Thank you for bringing me here, then."

I imagined we were back in that darkened room, all those weeks ago, sharing ourselves with each other.

"This is actually where I planned to propose to Diana, my ex. She wouldn't have enjoyed a picnic, but she would have liked the pictures we could have gotten here at sunset."

"What happened with her? I've picked up bits and pieces from your brothers, them being worried about our relationship because of your past with her." She spoke slowly, as if not to spook me.

"We met in grad school. Well, I was in grad school and she regularly went to the coffee shop down the street from the poli-sci building. It took me a month to work up the nerve to talk to her, but finally, the month before graduation, I did. I didn't know it at the time, but it turns out her taking up a post at that coffee shop was intentional. She fancied herself a politician's wife. Wanted to be the next Jackie O or something." I laughed at the irony of sitting here with a real life Jacqueline now, and she joined in.

"But she moved here with me when I left school."

"After a month?" Jax asked.

"Yup, after a month. She moved right into my first apartment. I added her to the lease and everything. I thought we were in love, but she just saw me as her ticket to the life she wanted. But there was a reason she was still coming to the coffee shop at the end of the year. She was beautiful, but didn't know a thing about politics or history.

"Everyone else saw right through her, but I guess I just wanted a partner and figured it would keep my work life separate from my home life. Anyway, I planned to propose after just a few months, but Duncan found out she was scheming to get me to run for office sooner. She wasn't happy with me wanting to work as a staffer for a while. She wanted things to get moving. She was here, why should she have to wait?"

"Oh, Preston, I'm so sorry."

I shrugged. Even though I had been alone ever since, I was over Diana and her betrayal. "Because she was on the lease, she had claim to the apartment and refused to move out. Last I heard, she had hitched her wagon to a guy on some twenty-four-hour news channel. A more glamorous life, I guess.

"I broke the lease and moved back home with my dad and worked in local government back in Massachusetts for a while. Being back in New England is how I found Senator Marsden, started working for his campaign, and ended up here. So it's not all bad."

Jax looked out over those crowds climbing the steps to the monument before turning back to me. "Why in the world did you ever agree to be fake engaged to me? I think one of my selling points was that it would look good for you to have a partner when you ran for office. God, you should have gone running the other way."

I met her eyes. "Maybe it was because you were no games right from the start. You presented that part as a benefit, not as some surprise secret plan you'd hidden." I took a deep breath, taking a risk, my heart feeling like it might pound out of my chest. "And I don't know. Maybe even then, at that very first dinner, I could tell you were someone I could fall in love with."

CHAPTER

Twenty

JAX

I sat there, stunned by Preston's revelation. I knew I should say something, but how do you respond to someone who just told you they saw so much in you?

But was I really surprised? These past few weeks, I could tell Preston's feelings had changed, but he held them back. I didn't want to call him on it, because that might force me to admit I liked the way we were. I liked Preston. I liked the person I was with him.

"Ha. So that's how it feels to have a heartfelt declaration met with silence. It's not great." Preston started to pack up our food.

"Wait." I put my hand on his arm. "Do you want to know what I work on late at night?"

He looked at me confused, as if his patience was wearing thin.

"I know, I know. But I promise, it's related."

He sat back down, resting his arms on his bent knees. "Okay, I'll bite. What are you working on late at night?"

"Well, you know I moved in with my grandma after my parents died."

"So you're communicating with the great beyond?" He

clenched his fists. "Sorry, that's not fair. I know . . . well, you know I know at least a fraction of how it feels to lose someone. I'm just lashing out."

"I'm a champion lasher-outer. I know. But thank you for apologizing." I waited a beat, and then continued.

"Right after the accident, I had a lot of trouble sleeping. My grandma was a voracious Harlequin serials reader, and I had moved into her library. It was the only other room in the house. I started reading these books until the early morning.

"They probably weren't all appropriate for a sixteen-year-old, but they helped some with the nightmares, so my grandma didn't take them away. Soon the familiar pattern of the Happy Ever After, the rhythms these stories took, became a comfort to me. I decided I wanted to write romance novels."

"That's what you focused on for your MFA," Preston said, the lightbulb clicking on in his head.

I nodded. "Yes. My grandma loved that we shared a passion for these stories. She would tell everyone her granddaughter was going to be the next Nora Roberts." I laughed, unsurprised when it sounded a bit wet. "She died after a brief illness my senior year of college. I had already been accepted to my MFA program, so she knew I was on the path to our dream. She left me some money, enough to help cover tuition and get me started. I was going to do it for her."

"So, what happened?" Preston's face read open and caring now, so unlike the closed off, hurt man of a few moments ago. His ability to put aside his own emotions and pain, to focus on someone else, made *me* want to care for *him*. Who put him first?

"Well, some bill collectors came out of the woodwork and found me. I was all alone—I had no other family I could turn to. Looking back, there were probably resources to fight it, but I just wanted it to be over, to stop drudging up the pain that my grandma was *gone*. As if I wasn't aware of that fact every day."

"So you paid them," he said, his voice full of sorrow.

"I did. And it took every dollar I had, and then some, making installments with jobs I worked during grad school. I missed out on making connections with my cohort, because I was always working or catching up on schoolwork. But my grandma's memory pushed me to keep going.

"I needed some way to make money after graduation and the best man at my parent's wedding had a connection in political reporting, so I took it. He tried to check in on me afterward, but I felt so ashamed of accepting his help I dodged his calls and eventually he stopped trying."

We sat there in silence for a moment, before Preston broke it. "So the late-night work?"

"It took about three months of being a low-level reporter for me to realize I was going to lose my soul and my mind if I didn't find another outlet. So, I set up a pen name and started publishing romance novels. I wanted to keep my identity a secret, so I would be taken seriously in my day job.

"I've published ten novels over the last five years. I feel just on the cusp of making it, being able to write full time, but I keep having these setbacks. A paper will close, or a temp job will end, or I'll need to find somewhere new to live. The books get done, but the rest of it—the marketing, the outreach—falls away. Because it's just me. I'm on my own."

Preston scooted over so he was next to me, reaching out hesitantly to take my hand. "Do you want to be on your own?"

I looked down at our fingers, how they fit together. How *we* fit together. Two people who started essentially as strangers in four hundred square feet. "I haven't tried it another way for a long, long time."

We sat, gazing into the bright afternoon sunlight. I saw the families walking around the reflection pool—brothers chasing sisters, teenagers pretending they were too cool for a family trip. I watched people running, checking their watches as they rounded the bend to the next part of their route. Were they checking a message from someone they were hurrying to get home to? Even the eccentric man spouting philosophically about the end times from a folding chair gathered attention, if for just a fleeting moment.

"I write happy-ever-afters, but there are no guarantees in life. People change. People *leave*."

"I know." Preston wrapped his arm around me, tucking me into his side. I leaned my head on his shoulder. Even my skittish heart couldn't deny the way this felt right. "I get scared too. But I think what I've realized over the past two months is that I'm even more scared not to try."

We sat like that, watching as the shadows changed and the clouds moved by. Nothing ever stayed the same, but in new light, things remained beautiful.

Neither of us had the energy to bike, so we caught a ride share back to Eastern Market, where Preston dropped the bag and reusable containers off in a box left for just that purpose. As we turned to continue on, I said, "I can't decide if I want a cup of hot chocolate, a shower, or a nap when we get home."

Preston stopped in his tracks, his fingers slipping from mine after his stalled momentum pulled on my arm.

"What? What's wrong?"

He looked at me, eyes wide in trepidation. "You called it home."

I played back the moment as my hand touched my lips, as if I could trace the words I uttered. It was a small thing, removing the word home from my vocabulary. Back to "my place," or "my sublet," or even "my pad" when things got really wacky. But never home.

With eyes wide, I dropped my hand from my mouth to reveal a smile, my gaze catching his. Preston took two giant steps forward and captured me in a fierce embrace. His mouth came down on mine as if only my lips could provide his oxygen, like a diver resurfacing for air. I wrapped my arms around his neck, squealing into the kiss as his grip pulled me off my feet.

The kiss slowed, and I grabbed either side of his face, keeping us nose to nose. "Let's go home."

We somehow made it through the door of our apartment in one piece, knowing an indecent exposure charge wouldn't help anyone.

"Too. Many. Buttons," I said, working at his shirt, meeting his eyes with a smirk before—*riiippp*—I popped those buttons right loose.

"I thought you said that was harder than it looked," Preston said as he wrestled with my jeans.

"I guess I just needed the right motivation." I helped him push my jeans down my legs, stumbling as I tried to step out before my feet were free.

"Whoa there, steady. Concussions and sex don't mix," he joked. His voice sounded lighter than it had in days. I hated his feelings had been dragging him down. I wanted to help fix that.

"So," he said, running his fingers up my sides, under my shirt. I shivered at the touch. "Do you still want hot chocolate? A shower? A nap?"

"I'm not ruling out the need for a nap. But later." I bent down to bite his nipple, earning a hiss in response.

"Okay. Bed. Now." He picked me up, hands cupping my ass, forcing my legs around his waist. The rough fabric of his jeans rubbed against my thigh. These would need to go. I tried to reach between us to undo his button and zipper.

"Whoa," he said, taking three more steps with me firmly crushed against his body before dumping me on the bed. "The apartment's small, but I still can't magically transport from one spot to another. I don't want to drop you."

"So particular with not wanting to drop your fiancée," I

joked, trying to use my feet to push his jeans down his hips and off. He helped me, finishing the job and taking his boxer briefs with it. His cock slapped against his stomach as he stood back up, and he grabbed it in one hand, giving it a few quick strokes, catching a bead of wetness from the tip on his finger.

"Gimme," I said, opening my mouth, clamping down on his finger as I sucked the drop of precum clean. My tongue swirled around the tip of his finger for good measure, earning a guttural moan from where he leaned over the edge of the bed. He pulled his finger free with a pop, running the damp finger down my collarbone and circling my nipple, tightening the already hard bud into a tall point.

"God, you're beautiful." Preston stood with one foot on the floor, the other kneeling on the bed next to my legs. I felt like I could float away without his weight to ground me.

"I need you inside me, please," I said, scrambling with my fingers on his skin, trying to gain purchase to pull him onto me. He put one knee on each side of my hips, his cock pressed into my stomach as he leaned down to give me a slow, yet sinful kiss.

"Since you said please." He pushed off to lean for his bedside drawer.

"Wait," I stopped him. "I was tested at the beginning of the year and my results were negative. And I have an IUD. I haven't been with anyone since then but you."

"I get screened every year at my PCP. I think she thought I was lying when I said I wasn't sexually active. But my results were negative as well. Do you want to?"

I bit my lip, nodding. "I just want you."

Preston's eyes shut tight, absorbing those words. When they opened again, I could see a pool of care and affection aimed right at me.

I tilted my hips up, opening for him. My hand reached for the base of his cock and his encircled mine. Together, we guided him inside. He slid right home, slowly but firmly, the stretch and burn turning to fullness in an instant.

Pressing a kiss to each cheek, Preston held himself aloft over me and started to move his hips. He moved in slow grinding strokes, the root of his cock grinding over my clit with each stroke. "Oh, fuck," I murmured as I wrapped my legs tighter around his waist. I dreaded the emptiness I would feel if he left me, left my center, so I pulled tight to keep him close.

Gradually, the slow pace of his thrusts increased as he started to thrust harder and deeper. My legs started to shake, beginning to slip from their perch on his hips. One side at a time, he slid my legs down so my foot was planted flat on the bed.

Wrapping one arm under my back, he angled my hips up slightly. His thrusts grew near frantic in nature, bottoming out with each stroke. The new angle still stroked my clit while hitting deep inside me, and a wave began to crest inside me.

Preston picked his head up, meeting my eyes for a moment before his lips sealed to mine. "I'm close," he said against my lips. "God, you feel so perfect. You're perfect. *We're* perfect."

My orgasm blinded me, the wave breaking without warning and I felt myself cry out against his mouth, biting down on his lower lip. Preston's thrusts stuttered as he fought to stroke through my pussy clenching around him, eventually burying himself deep with his head in my neck.

We lie like that, breathing heavily, his hand stroking my hair while mine rubbed in time on his back.

"Hey," he said, looking up. "Are you okay? Shit, I didn't hurt you, did I?" He wiped under my eye, alerting me that tears had spilled over. "Did I bite you? So, you bit me back? Ugh, I ruined it." He looked so sated and devastated at the same time. It was adorable and yet needed to be fixed immediately.

I shook my head, trying to find my words. "You didn't ruin anything. You're so good. It's you. You're the reason why this is home." I reached up to kiss him gently, mindful of his lip.

We kissed slowly for a while before Preston rolled off me. He walked to the bathroom and came back with a wet cloth. He cleaned me up gently, before wiping himself off and throwing the washcloth onto the floor.

"You're going to regret that later," I teased, as he pulled me into his side and we watched the sun set outside the window.

"Probably. Worth it." He pressed a kiss to my forehead.

"So," he continued. "Turns out you have an emotional intimacy kink."

I laughed. "I'm not quite sure that qualifies as a kink, but you're right. Turns out emotional intimacy isn't exactly a bad thing."

"Look at that. I taught *you* something in the bedroom."

I rolled my eyes as he squeezed me closer, arranging my limbs half on top of his.

"I could go for that hot chocolate now," I said. The chilly evening April air cooled the apartment from the window we left open now that the sun had disappeared.

"Give me five minutes and I'll see what I can do." We lay there in silence as Preston's breathing evened out, falling asleep. I shut my eyes as I pulled the comforter tight around us. We'd regret this nap in the morning, but we'd deal with whatever tomorrow brings. Together.

CHAPTER
Twenty~One

PRESTON

I felt on top of the world. The senator's poll numbers were strong and climbing every week. My mood seemed contagious, I think I even caught him laughing at one of Laurel's jokes in a staff meeting yesterday.

We were experiencing the few weeks of true spring in DC before we rounded the bend into flat-out summer. Longer days for once didn't mean more time to be at the office, because it took longer to get dark to signal me to go home. Instead, they meant time to walk outside with Jax, eating dinner at outdoor restaurants with Jax, pretending to watch baseball games at Nats Park with Hayden, Charlotte, and Jax, and well, essentially just be with Jax.

Sure, we still had some things to figure out. The three-month deadline we set for our initial fake engagement was looming. We admitted these feelings were real, that they were worth exploring. Did that mean we stayed "engaged" while we dated and hope we decided we wanted to take that leap for real? All great questions that were a perfect problem for future Preston. Current me found myself happier than I could remember being in a long, long time.

Jax and I were enjoying the weather tonight by participating in a Senate vs. House staffers softball league on the National Mall. The New England Senate team had come in second last season, and we were out for blood.

Jax hadn't been too keen on playing in the first place, wanting to sit with Laurel and heckle while drinking wine out of a Thermos, but I found a way to persuade her. I may not have come into our relationship with much sexual experience, but I now found myself very fluent in reading Jax's body. A few well-placed orgasms went a long way to convincing her to join the team, though she promised retribution in kind on something in the future. I looked forward to her making her case.

"C'mon, Jax!" I yelled from second base. It was the bottom of the final inning of the first week of games. Two outs, and the score was tied. If Jax could hit me home, we'd win. I never considered myself an overly competitive person, but growing up with four brothers inevitably instilled some competitive urges deep inside you, and something about work league softball brought them out.

Laurel woo-hooed from her spot on the grass behind home plate, waving her Thermos in the air as Jax swung and missed the first pitch. Everyone enjoyed sports in different ways. Jax asked for a time out, stepping back from the plate, and took a few more practice swings.

"You got this baby!" I yelled, really taking it over the top, but my gut was starting to twist. She would take being the final out hard, and she only signed up because of my encouragement.

She stepped back up to the plate, swung hard at the pitch, and sent the ball flying over my head. As soon as she made contact, I took off and made it home before the ball even got back to the infield. Jax stood on first base, jumping up and down while the rest of the team cheered. The Housers looked a bit dejected, but also ready to head out and start drinking.

I took off down the first base line toward Jax, and she met me halfway, jumping into my arms. I spun her around, her arms and legs out in celebration, before I pulled her head down to mine. Forgetting these were our colleagues for a second, we kissed until Laurel's wolf whistle pierced my consciousness, breaking the moment.

"I think I like softball after all," Jax said, sliding down my body. She bent down and put the hat back on my head she had knocked off during our enthusiastic celebrations.

"See, I knew you'd have fun." I wrapped my arm around Jax's waist and we headed toward Laurel's blanket to grab our stuff.

"I reserve the right to change my mind as soon as we start losing though. It's only fun when you're on top."

"I think it's fun when you're on top too," I said into her ear in a low voice.

"Dirty talk? Who knew Preston had it in him," Laurel said, smirking up at me, her hand shading the setting sun. Apparently not a low enough voice.

"Anything left in that Thermos?" I asked, hoping any redness in my face could be chalked up to in-game exertion.

She shook it, the sound of liquid answering the question.

"Gimme," Jax said, reaching out and taking a big swig, finishing what remained.

"You guys are going out with everyone, right?" Laurel asked, screwing the top back on the Thermos and picking up her blanket to fold. I grabbed the other end to make the job easier.

"Nope," Jax said. "We have an errand to run."

"And you didn't save any wine for me to make it go down easier," I complained.

"We're going to buy Preston a new suit tonight, so he has it for his tailoring appointment tomorrow, so it can be ready for his new headshots on Saturday," Jax explained. "We wouldn't have to do this tonight if someone had wanted to go shopping any time I suggested it since we made the appointment with the photographer, but he didn't. So tonight is crunch time."

"Maybe someone would have wanted to go shopping for suits if someone else didn't make such a compelling argument to stay home, in bed." I figured I might as well go for broke since Laurel already caught us.

"Y'all are cute. And gross. But I now feel bad for people who are around when Caitlin and I do this. A real effective emotional tornado you two have whipped up. Time to go drink." With that, Laurel waved to us over her shoulder and walked off to join the staff from a Maine senator's office.

"All right, buddy, no more stalling. Off we go." Jax pushed me to start walking toward the Macy's located a few blocks from the White House.

"As far as pet names go, not crazy about buddy," I said, falling into step beside her as we crossed Constitution and headed up 12th Street.

"Yeah, that wasn't a pet name. That was condescension," she replied, trying and failing to keep a straight face. We stopped at an intersection, waiting for a walk sign, and I pulled her in close, pressing a kiss to her forehead while she rested her chin on my chest. Once we got our signal, we separated, but I moved to tangle my hand with hers, grinning when I felt her reaching for my hand right back.

"Are you going to be okay, foodwise?" I asked. "I know you didn't eat much before the game."

"Yeah." she nodded. "I had a little something because I knew I could run into a museum if I needed to. I have a protein bar in my bag. I'll munch on it while you're modeling for me."

"Here's an idea," I said as we reached the store, the blast of air conditioning feeling good after our walk. "What if you picked out a new dress, too?"

She shot me a confused look. "I don't need a new dress for anything."

"What about your book release next month?"

"I mean, I don't really do much for a book release. Since I don't associate my face with my pen name, it's not like I can do a launch event or anything."

"I know," I said, gesturing for her to get on the escalator

toward the men's department ahead of me. "But I thought we could go out for a nice dinner or something. You could wear a new dress, we could drink champagne, make a night of it."

She stepped off the escalator, standing in front of the store map. I would bet she wasn't actually reading it. "I've never celebrated a book release before."

I stepped up behind her. "I'd be happy to be your first." She leaned back against me for a moment, in a way I knew showed her appreciation.

"Okay, fine, but only if we find a suit you like in time. I'm not giving up playing dress-up with my very own Preston doll."

I rolled my eyes. I wore a suit almost every day to work, yes, but I never put much thought into colors or how they fit. As long as they weren't too tight or too baggy or too khaki, they were fine. Jax wanted me to get a new suit for these headshots. She had visions of them accompanying my campaign announcement. We had plenty of time between now and then, but a photographer friend she knew had an opening this weekend and would do it for cheap, so here we were.

"Okay, so we definitely want to do a navy one—to bring out your eyes." Jax started rifling through the racks. "A classic black and a nice charcoal will be good options too. You're sure I can't talk you into multiple suits and an outfit change for Saturday?"

I stared at her deadpan. "One suit. No changing."

"Okay, okay," she said, hoisting up a pile of suits I hadn't even noticed her picking out.

"How do you know my size?"

Now she stared at me with a lack of amusement. "We sleep in the same bed, buddy. I'm pretty sure that means I'm entitled to go through your closet to get your pants and jacket sizes." She took off toward the dressing room, calling over her shoulder. "We'll start with these."

I supposed I was meant to follow her, so I started moving. "Still not a big fan of the buddy."

"Noted!"

Twenty minutes later we had a pile of no's, a few maybes, and one suit left to try on.

"Isn't this the navy one you picked out first?" I asked from behind the dressing room door.

"Yes, but it was my favorite from the rack, so I wanted it to be last."

"That's diabolical. Why couldn't it have been first and we could have saved a ton of our time and *my* energy?" I said, opening the door.

"Because, this way, we'll know it's really . . ." her words trailed off as she looked over at me. "Yup, that's the one. I want to tear it right off you, more so than any of the others."

I laughed. "Quite a scale you've developed there." I walked to the three-way mirror to check this suit out, and had to agree, the look worked.

I saw her shrug in the reflection. "When it works, it works. What do you think?"

"I think we have a winner. I still wish we would have started with this one, but I won't question the process anymore." I looked at my smartwatch. "And we still have time to look at a dress for you."

Jax met me in front of my changing room. "Or, I could help you get out of that suit. Make sure it stays neat for the tailor tomorrow . . ."

I leaned in to kiss her, waiting for her eyes to close before pulling back and slamming the door in her face.

"Preston!"

"Nice try, but you're looking at dresses."

"Fine," she said and stomped off to sit down in her chair.

After I changed back into my softball gear, we made our way to the third floor where the dress section was. Jax started to flick through the racks with less enthusiasm than I expected.

"If you don't want to do this, we don't have to. It was just an idea."

Jax sighed. "No, it's a really sweet idea. You're the nicest for thinking of it and wanting to help me celebrate. It's just . . . I've been thinking for a while, I wish I could claim my books. I don't write them for any accolades or recognition, but I would love to meet my readers face-to-face at an event or chat with an aspiring author about their dreams."

"Well, could you? I know you told the senator you're a romance author, and moving right past the fact you told him before me"—she stuck her tongue out at me—"if there's any part of you that cares about what I think you should do, I would be proud to support you chasing your dream as Jacqueline Carter."

She started at the rack in concentration, not saying anything.

"How about this?" I asked softly. "You pick out a dress for a dinner to celebrate this book, just us. If you decide in the future to claim your pen name, you can reuse it for a book signing."

"You wouldn't buy me a second dress? Cheapskate," she said, her face lighter than moments before.

I laughed. "I'll buy you as many dresses as you, and my political salary, will let me."

"Hmm. Good point. Does Duncan like buying women dresses?"

"Okay, joke time's over," I said, starting to go through the racks myself. I knew she was just kidding, but the thought of anyone else, even my brother, buying this woman a dress raised my blood pressure. "Do I get to pick out things for you to try on this time?"

Jax shook her head. "Nope. I think I have the winner right here." A flash of blue fabric appeared before she draped it over her arm. "But I think you'll see you did influence it somewhat." She took off in search of a dressing room.

"Wait, so you get to just try on one, but I had to try on ten?" I half-yelled, following in her wake.

"Deal with it, buddy!"

Jax had already closed the changing room door by the time I reached the opening to the dressing room. I checked to be sure no one else was in there, not wanting to be the man who lurked in a dressing room uninvited. The door opened and she stepped out, taking my breath away. The dress had a peacock blue solid fabric that came to Jax's knees, with a low V-neck between her breasts, covered in lace that carried up over her shoulders.

"You like?" she asked, spinning so I could see the back, where the lace carried on, along her shoulders, leaving an open back.

I cleared my throat. "Wow. I love . . . love it. You look great."

She smiled shyly at me before turning back to the mirror. "It is a good dress. I hope it finds many uses from my closet over the years."

I stepped up behind her. "Think you need some help getting that off? That zipper looks hard to reach." I skimmed my fingers down her bare back.

"Shoppers, please make your final purchase. Macy's will be closing in ten minutes." While the announcement distracted me, Jax took the opening to close the door in my face. I groaned as Jax laughed. "Taste of your own medicine."

I knocked my head against the outer wall of the dressing room. "Hold that thought. We'll be home soon," she called, fabric rustling as she changed.

My heart still warmed every time she called the apartment home. Since she'd moved in, the word never felt more right.

BRANDT BROTHERS GROUP CHAT

SPENCER

Yo, Preston! You and Jax are on @HillStaffWatch. "Check out this link."

HAYDEN

Whoa, dude. PDA much?

HUNTER

Yeah, you're definitely one to talk.

HAYDEN

Can I come watch one of your games? I promise not to pants you this time.

DUNCAN

I'm honestly surprised Preston still plays softball.

PRESTON

Jax says I should invite you, Hayden, though I definitely still have PTSD. And Hunter's right. You're one to talk about PDA.

Also, Spencer, why do you follow @HillStaffWatch?

SPENCER

You're the one who sent us that list of 25 Best Butts on the Hill, complaining you weren't on it. You brought this on yourself.

PRESTON

That was like four years ago...

SPENCER

And? They do great listicles! Plus, I do scientific research sixty hours a week. I need gossip that didn't breed in a lab. Their stuff is gold.

DUNCAN

It was only a matter of time till you ended up on there, Prez. You've been getting a lot of attention since that school board speech.

They named Jax, too. Is she going to be okay with that?

HUNTER

She's engaged to a future politician. It was going to happen sooner or later.

HAYDEN

It's just @HillStaffWatch. Does anyone follow it but Congress staffers? And Spencer, apparently?

DUNCAN

It's good to be in the know.

PRESTON

I expected better from you of all people, Dunc.

Jax is right here and says her biggest regret is they're showing my ass in this picture and not hers. She wants a chance to make the list next year too, and thinks her big break was wasted.

HUNTER

She honestly might be perfect for you.

HAYDEN

For real.

PRESTON

I know.

CHAPTER
Twenty-Two

JAX

Preston and I strolled into the office at 10:00 a.m. on the second Monday in May after getting in late the night before from Rhode Island.

"Jaqueline! Preston! My office. Now," the senator bellowed as we were greeting Laurel.

"What's eating him?" I whispered to her, wondering if we could get a hint of what we were walking into.

"That was practically a guided invitation," Laurel whispered back. "He didn't even swear."

"True." I followed Preston down the hallway into Senator Marsden's office.

"Shut the door," he said when we were both in the room.

"What's going on, sir?" Preston asked, sliding into the chair next to me. Normally, I would have locked that away to make fun of him later, but the look on the senator's face had me thinking there wasn't much fun in my future.

"I got a heads up on an article running on *The Dispatch's* front page tomorrow. I thought you both would want to see it."

He handed two pieces of paper to Preston, who swore softly at whatever he saw. He looked over at me, his face pained.

"Give me the paper, Preston," I said, my tone firm. He handed it over reluctantly, his eyes on my face before going back to reading.

"Senator Marsden (RI) allows pornography author to run comms?" More vile bullshit followed, bringing in bathroom bills, women's rights, and other typical talking points of the paper's political leaning followed. But there, in plain, printed words, linked Jacqueline Carter to June Kennedy, my pen name.

Even worse, it linked Jacqueline Carter as the fiancée of Preston Brandt, seen engaging in "inappropriate" PDA at a congressional staffer's softball game. My eyes flicked to the byline on the article. No surprise here. Peggy Rappencourt had finally gotten one over on me. I wished I could say I regretted tangling with her, but I vehemently disagreed with her stances and her methods, like this.

"Well, fuck," I said.

"Well put," Mitchell said, folding his hands on the desk. "I already tried everything in my power to get the story killed. They're refusing. We only got a heads up on the article because I provided one of their interns with resources when his parents kicked him out of the house after they caught him with his boyfriend. The fucker has the wrong political beliefs, but I couldn't let him freeze."

I stared in wonder at my boss, realizing I never really knew what would come out of his mouth or go through his head.

"Okay, so, what now?" Preston said.

"Obviously, I quit and we break up," I said, staring at the words on the page until they blurred in front of my eyes, not wanting to look at either man in the room.

"Jax." I jumped as the senator used my nickname for the first time. "My campaign can weather this storm. It's a chance for me to talk about female empowerment, not judging sex workers, how the other side catastrophizes everything. We may take a small hit, but ultimately, it'll all even out. Certain people will eat this shit up. We may even gain a romance reader vote or two."

Preston laughed thinly, but I wasn't smiling. My eyes were only on Senator Marsden.

"And Preston?" I asked, reading the answer in his eyes already.

The senator glanced at Preston briefly, then returned his attention to me. "I have a reputation for being an asshole and taking no punches. I'm an incumbent senator with a solid lead in the polls. Preston is neither an asshole nor is he an incumbent anything. He will always have a place as my Chief of Staff for as long as he wants it."

I nodded, understanding what he wasn't saying. We couldn't predict exactly how this news would impact Preston's future career, but the chance it would be negative was real.

Unfortunately, Preston also read between the lines.

"I haven't even announced anything yet. We could see how things go. If it is a big storm, then I stay on here for a while. We both do. The House elects every two years. What's another 730 days?"

I threw my hands in the air, turning my body toward his. "That's ridiculous, and you know it. You're getting noticed. There's buzz around you running next election. You'd be stupid to waste it because of me."

"What if I don't think we're stupid," he said quietly, looking at his hands before turning his face toward mine. I saw in the depths of his eyes how much he believed in us, in me. I felt the world around me tunneling into a focal point on Preston's face. A roaring sounded in my ears. I couldn't be the reason he risked his dream, a dream instilled in him by his mom. I couldn't. I *wouldn't*.

"All right, this no longer seems like any of my concern. Jacqueline, I'm happy to have you stay, but I know you'll make your own decision."

Preston and I continued to look at each other, neither of us moving.

"Seriously. Get the fuck out."

We both jolted into motion, standing and heading to the door.

I turned back as Preston exited before me, and I saw something a lot like sympathy in Senator Marsden's eyes, before his asshole mask fell firmly back into place.

In the least surprising move of all time, Preston followed me to my desk. "We need to talk about this. I need to know you're not going to do something rash."

I hummed noncommittally. "I really can't talk about this right now. Can we get through the day and plan to reconvene at home tonight?" My gut roiled in revolt at my use of the word home. I knew it would appease Preston's anxieties for now and give me time to do exactly what he feared I would.

"After the softball game, right?"

I thunked my head on my desk in my mind. Fucking softball. "After the softball game."

He walked up to my desk and leaned over, giving me a soft kiss. "We're going to figure this out, babe. I promise."

Knocking on the top of my desk, he offered me another smile and went back to his own space.

"Sometimes there just isn't anything to figure out," I muttered. I turned on my computer, and got down to my new to-do list for the day, which had nothing to do with communications management for a senator's office.

Preston and the senator left for some engagement or another. I couldn't be bothered to check beyond me knowing it would have them out of the office for the rest of the afternoon. I gathered my stuff, walking out into the outer office with purpose, hoping I could fake it and sneak out unquestioned.

"Where are you going? You don't have any meetings this afternoon, and you have softball later. Are you okay?"

Damn those shared calendars and making friends with your coworkers. I turned to face Laurel.

"I'm great. I just forgot my tennis shoes at the apartment for this afternoon, so I'm going to run home and grab them."

"Your shoes are right there. I can see them bulging in the bottom of your bag." Laurel narrowed her eyes at me.

"Yes, but these are my dry weather tennis shoes. It looks like it might rain, so I need to go get my shoes that can get muddy." Not bad for talking out of my ass. Like I had more than one pair of tennis shoes meant for exercising.

"I didn't know it was supposed to rain." Laurel turned her attention to her computer, presumably to check the weather since there were no windows in this part of the office. I took my opportunity and slipped out the door, hearing her "Hey!" as I shut the door behind me.

Much in the way I arrived at Preston's, I left—my belongings in boxes and bags on a luggage cart. Life wasn't quite cruel enough to match me with the same ride share driver, and I helped the woman load everything into her SUV.

"Headed to Adams Morgan?" the driver asked.

"Yup," I responded, pulling out my phone to let Michelle know I was on my way and would be at her doorstep shortly.

Thirty minutes later, muddling through early rush hour traffic, I pulled up to Michelle's building. She met us at the street, and the ride share driver accepted an extra twenty dollars cash in tip to help us load everything on the elevator just inside the entryway.

"So," Michelle said, as she wiped sweat from her brow, putting the last of my boxes in her second bedroom. "Did you know before I decided to become a meteorologist, I was studying psychology?"

I looked at her for a beat. "No, you weren't."

She had the decency to look slightly chagrined. "Okay, no, I wasn't. But I'm an excellent listener. And the payment for harboring you in what feels like a slightly fugitive situation is the truth about what the fuck is happening."

I couldn't deny that was fair. "Okay, but I'm going to need some tacos and margaritas and confirmation you have a second bathroom because no matter the quality of Mexican food, it rarely agrees with me."

Michelle sprang into action. "You've got yourself a deal. I'm covering for the early morning meteorologist this week, so no margs for me, but the place next door does to go. Their food's shit on weekdays. The weekend chef is much better, so we'll get food from District Taco. Here, pick what you want."

It was nice for someone else to take charge of my life for a few moments, even though I knew the consequences of my actions would come raining down on me sooner rather than later. I checked the time, noting the game should be starting soon, and Preston would realize I wasn't going to show.

I couldn't let him risk everything because of me, or worse, resent me in a few years when he looked back and realized what his life could have been. Tears trickled out of my eyes when I realized I pictured a life with Preston years down the line. All that was about to be wiped out because I liked to write dirty scenes in books about love and a humongous grudge from an awful woman.

I shook my head, wiping my tears. The actions of others wouldn't dictate how I felt about my books. I loved writing. She and everyone who agreed with her were the ones who were wrong.

My inhale was a bit shaky and louder than I meant it to be, causing Michelle to look up in alarm. "Okay, I'm adding an extra order of chips and queso. We are about to get into it."

I laughed, laying back on her couch, hugging a pillow to my stomach. Learning to open myself up to Preston allowed me to make true friends for the first time in my adult life. Never did I think I would be this grateful to have somewhere to turn. If I couldn't have Preston, at least I wasn't completely alone.

CHAPTER
Twenty-Three

PRESTON

I've never played a worse game of softball. Every female figure who walked near the game caught my gaze, just in case they were Jax showing up with a smile and a story. In retrospect, I should have left when she was fifteen minutes late and hadn't answered my three phone calls or Laurel's two more after the game had started. I just kept expecting her to show up, with some explanation for her delay and a smile flashed my way. All my worries forgotten.

Except my worries grew and grew. As soon as the other team recorded the final out, handing us a loss, I jogged off the field. Laurel handed me my stuff. "I kept trying to get ahold of her. She said she needed to go home to grab a different pair of sneakers this afternoon. I'm sure she's fine."

I nodded, unable to consider anything else. I jogged the whole way from the field to our place, not able to remember the journey or if I stopped to wait for walk signals like I should have. I jammed my finger on the elevator button, trying to tell myself Jax would be waiting on the sixth floor for me. The sinking feeling in my gut told me otherwise.

I tried the door, finding it locked and dug my keys out. "Jax?"

I called, finally getting the door open, throwing it against the wall with too much force. We'd laugh about that dent later, right?

I spun around in the middle of the room, as if I expected her to pop up out of a corner when I faced the right direction. On the second rotation, the bright white of the bed caught my eye. The blues and purples from Jax's quilt were gone.

"No, no, no," I said, rushing over to the dresser and pulling open her drawer. Empty. I wheeled around, looking at her bedside table. The outlines of dust from where her stack of books sat stared me in the face. I grabbed my hair, pulling on it, trying to engage my brain to think, to understand.

That's when I saw it. A blue velvet box in front of the TV. I walked over and picked it up, my hands trembling. The engagement ring sat nestled inside. I snapped the box closed, clutching it in my fist before setting it back on the TV stand.

When I gave the ring to Jax three months ago, I didn't think anyone would ever wear it for real. That I'd ever want to open myself up again. But boy, did Jax prove me wrong. That ring belonged on her finger. Maybe not now in this fake, set up sort of way. She was it for me. I just needed to make her see it too.

But first, I had to find her.

I pulled out my phone and dialed Hayden's number. Why she would leave me without any clues to her whereabouts and tell my brother, I had no idea. But I needed to start somewhere.

Hayden answered, sounding distracted. "Hey man, what's up?"

"Have you seen Jax?"

"No? Should I have?" I heard what sounded like the fridge opening, a glass clinking.

"Do you know if she's texted or called Charlotte?"

"Charlotte's gone this week, visiting a store outside Pittsburgh. Oh, that reminds me, can you ask Jax what that margarita place is her friend Michelle likes? I guess she told Charlotte about it and Charlotte's dying to go. Thought I'd surprise her when she gets back."

I rolled my eyes at how off topic Hayden got so quickly, obviously not picking up on my distress. But he was also a genius, because now I knew exactly where Jax fled.

"Yeah, sure thing. I'll make that my first priority when I find her. Okay, gotta go now."

"Wait!"

Hayden's voice blared through the phone. I put it on speaker so I could talk and move at the same time.

"Yeah?"

"What do you mean when you find her? What's going on?"

I let out a scream-groan of frustration.

"Jax has a secret identity that's going to get revealed tomorrow. There's a possibility it could be a strike against any future political career I have. I thought we were going to talk things over tonight. Instead, when I got home, she and all of her stuff were gone."

"Wait, so she's like a spy?"

Could I reach through the phone and strangle someone? I stopped to consider, pants half on.

"No, you numbskull. It's her secret to tell and the whole world is going to know tomorrow, so I'd rather not participate in that, which I know is dumb, but I just . . ." I stood in the middle of my apartment, one pant leg on, shirt off, not sure what to do next, feeling like I might cry.

"Preston. Just breathe. Do you know where she is?" Hayden's voice sounded calming and concerned.

"I think she's at Michelle's. She doesn't have a ton of places she could go. So I'm going over there now to try to talk some sense into her." My words shocked me back into action. Maybe I should have showered first? No time.

"Prez, wait. I know you want to see her. I can only imagine if I got home and Charlotte's stuff was gone and I wasn't one-hundred percent sure where she was . . . Well, I'd want to burn the whole world down too. But if she left without saying anything, she probably needs some time."

I started to make sounds of protest, but he continued.

"No, I know. I'm not saying days or weeks. Just hours. Give her tonight. Besides, it's almost dark and you're not positive she's there. You can't just roll up at a woman's place and try to break down the door after dark."

I sat on the edge of the bed, staring out the window, not truly seeing the setting sun.

"You're right."

"When you're feeling better, we're going to return to this momentous occasion of you admitting I'm right. But for now, do you need anything?"

I sucked in a big breath. "Would you . . . would you come over? I'd rather not be alone right now, and maybe you can help me sort through things and figure out what to say?"

"Pretty sure speech writing is your wheelhouse, big bro, but of course. I'll be right there. Have you eaten? Doesn't matter. I'm bringing food. And beer. But only two each. You need to be ready to go win back your girl in the a.m."

Hayden hung up without saying goodbye, clearly intent on accomplishing his to-do list and getting over here. Ironic he pointed out what I asked for help with essentially equated to writing a speech, but I felt all out of words when faced with the monumental stakes of the occasion.

I picked up my phone again, and opened to my text thread with Jax, wincing at all the unanswered messages from my side of the conversation.

PRESTON

Can you please let me know you're safe?

The dots indicating someone was typing appeared almost immediately.

JAX

I'm safe

I stared at my phone for a few moments longer, willing the dots to appear again, for Jax to tell me a little bit more. Tell me she missed me, just as much as I missed her. That she trusted me to stand by her, weather any storm to come our way, now and in the future. She meant too much to me to just shake off and move on. A box left on the TV stand, closed like the end of a story. Our story. This couldn't be the end.

The phone screen stayed stagnant, and I clicked it off. I hoped Hayden got here soon. It turned out I was hungry . . . and ready to bring my woman home.

Hayden made me promise I would wait until 9:00 a.m. before ringing Michelle's buzzer. So naturally, I arrived at her address, which I had wormed out of Laurel with obscene promises I'm not sure I ever had a shot in hell to fulfill, by eight-thirty. I waited at a coffee shop down the street, deciding loitering brought more of a creepy vibe than I was willing to take on. Taking a deep breath, I checked on the article. Maybe no one wanted to read this morning.

Somehow, the article was already trending on *The Dispatch's* website. Okay. Everyone wanted to read this morning. It looked like Buzzfeed picked it up as well. The comment section on *The Dispatch* was unsurprising, but made me sick nonetheless. I clicked over to the Buzzfeed article, hoping for better results. The title made me pause. "Why Are We So Afraid of Women's Sexual Empowerment?" That sounded promising. I read on.

The article didn't even mention me or Senator Marsden by name. It laid out the situation, Jax being allegedly tied to a pen name against her will. She worked for a political campaign, and she was engaged to someone with political aspirations.

But from there, it spun off in a different direction, discussing the history of the romance industry and the lack of respect it got from the literary world and larger world beyond. Experts were quoted, other articles were linked. It was an incredibly thorough article for something that only went live a handful of hours ago.

I scrolled back to the top of the article and recognized the top contributing writer's name, Katie Beck as a source our office used when the senator wanted something discussed in the more mainstream media. Had he . . . the only way this would have been put together in time was if Katie was given a heads up *The Dispatch* article was coming. *Interesting.*

The article finished by saying whether Jax was June Kennedy or not, writers deserved their privacy for a whole variety of reasons, and to check out one of their books. The comment section here was much more positive. Some hateful vitriol still mixed in, especially because some of Jax's books featured same-sex couples as the leads. Most excitingly, it was full of people saying they were planning to check out Jax's books and share them with other romance-loving friends.

The alarm I set for 8:58 a.m. went off, and I drained the last of my coffee, energized to see Jax. My phone vibrated again, and I looked to see a message from Charlotte.

CHARLOTTE

Hayden filled me in a bit about what happened. Hope you get to talk to Jax today.

If you do, make sure you show her this. At least half a dozen people have already sent me the Buzzfeed link today, without even knowing I know Jax.

The link Charlotte included led to Jax's Amazon author page. I clicked over and saw several of her books were in the top 100 of their categories, and one charted in the top 100 of the entire Kindle store. If Jax wanted it, that open, successful career she dreamed of was within reach.

The resolve inside my body thickened like a lightning bolt to the heart. I wasn't an idealist. You couldn't have a career in politics and remain one completely. But I believed this situation wasn't as dire as Jax seemed determined to make it to be. If nothing else, she needed to grab this opportunity by the horns for herself.

I hit the buzzer for apartment 2D, with no response. I jammed it again and again, recognizing I approached on nuisance status. Maybe she wasn't here? When did Michelle leave for work?

I tried one more time, leaving the button depressed much longer than socially acceptable. Then I heard it, a tinny voice.

"Michelle Hammond's apartment?" She sounded uncertain and little annoyed.

"Jax. It's me."

"Oh."

Silence echoed through the vestibule as loudly as a jet engine taking off. I hit the button again.

"Please let me up."

More silence, before a soft, "Okay," accompanied by a buzzing noise, unlocking the door so I could enter.

The door to 2D sat cracked open slightly. I knocked and pushed the door open, spotting Jax pacing back and forth through the living room.

"Hey," I said, shoving my hands in my pockets to keep from reaching out for her. Seeing her acted as a balm for the part of me terrified since I realized she left. Anger and anxiety also churned in my gut—hurt that she would leave without talking to me and worry nothing I said would make a difference.

"Hi," she said, stopping in her movements and turning to face me. Her eyes had dark shadows under them from lack of sleep, and her lip was red and swollen from her teeth. I wanted to bite that lip.

"How did you find me?" she asked, her arms wrapping around her midsection.

"Hayden mentioned margaritas last night, and I realized Michelle's place was the most likely place for you to go. You probably looked for other sublets yesterday, but the idea of dealing with strangers felt too much, so you ran to the one familiar place you could."

"Ha," she laughed, the sound cold and void of emotion. "So you've got me all figured out. I assume you've got a solution to our situation all figured out, too. Does it matter what I want?"

"What?" I said, honestly bewildered. "Of course it matters what you want. If you really believe we have no way forward, then I'll leave you alone. But I don't believe that's what you want. I wanted the chance to talk with you and figure something out together. That's what hurt the most. You didn't trust me to talk things through, to count on me to know myself and support you at the same time."

"I don't want you to resent me." She burst out. "It's easier to just end it now. That way you can have the career you want, achieve your goals, and I won't stand in your way. I can't be the reason you don't succeed in the dreams you inherited from your mom. You can't put that on me." Jax's voice broke at the mention of my mom, tears streaming down her face.

It physically pained me to not go to her. I put as much emotion into my voice as I could, wanting to make it impossible for her to not meet my eyes.

"Do you know what else I got from my mom? The idea that our family, our people are important. That's why she cared about politics, about supporting causes. It was all about the people. I've lived twice as long without her as I did with her, but I'm certain she'd be so pissed at me if I let you go just because of a little hardship. There are lots of ways I can achieve the dream she left me. There are not a lot of ways I can imagine a happy life without you in it."

I breathed heavily, like I had run a marathon. The surety I had in my words warmed me from the center, fighting away the cold dread of Jax's distance. Now all I could do was wait to see if she believed me.

CHAPTER
Twenty~Four

JAX

"There are not a lot of ways I can imagine a happy life without you in it."

I stared at Preston, stunned. Running away from real connection had been my way of life for so long. Keeping things superficial with coworkers or temporary roommates. Losing my parents and then losing Grandma, being left on my own. Those losses created a hurt I never wanted to feel again. While it hurt to think of losing Preston now, the thought of him deciding I was no longer worth the sacrifice, worth the effort, would break me to a point I might never recover from.

"You're just saying that. It's only been twelve hours. We're not even sure what the fallout from the article will be. I'm sure in a few days . . ."

Preston crossed the room, gripping my arms in his hands. He held on tightly for a second, like he needed to be sure I was real and standing here. He loosened his grip, making sure I knew I could step away in an instant if I needed to. I could sense the effort it took to stop himself from touching me earlier and felt something ease inside me at his touch.

"We can't know what the future holds. And I understand

that's terrifying. We both know that the people we love can be taken from us in an instant. I'm sorry you'll never meet my mom, and I'll never meet your parents or grandma. But the way you care about me . . ."

I opened my mouth to protest. He silenced me, putting a finger on my lips.

"I know you care a whole lot, Jax. You wouldn't have run if you didn't. But I'm certain they wouldn't have wanted you to close yourself off from caring about and being cared for by others, just because of a fear you could lose them. We have a chance to chase our dreams. Have a happy-ever-after, like the ones you write in your books. I'd love for us to do it together."

My face drew down in confusion. "I mean, I know the senator said I could keep my job, but I'm not really sure that's my dream. Though it's been lovely working there." I got that last part out in a rush.

Preston chuckled. "Have you looked online at all since the story broke this morning?"

I shook my head. "I stuffed my phone between the couch cushions to stop myself from doom scrolling. I can handle the things they've said about me. I've been navigating my bad reviews for years. It was negative things about you I wanted to avoid."

The smile that took over his face told me he saw to the heart of me. That he had crawled in through the cracks and crevices in the walls I built to keep people out. He filled those weak spots with care and kindness to help keep me protected, at the same time unlocking the door to allow those with the password to filter in and out freely. "I think you should go grab your phone. And check your Amazon author dashboard."

I looked at him skeptically, but went over to the couch and retrieved my phone, anyway. Messages and notifications filled the screen, but I ignored those and navigated to the browser I kept open on my sales ranks. My eyes widened as I took in the high rankings for many of my titles. Hands shaking, I looked at the sales info page. My eyes filled with tears for the second time this morning when I saw the order number on the page, climbing with each refresh. How was this possible?

My eyes met Preston's, holding so many questions. He beamed at me. "I have a sneaking suspicion, that will probably never be confirmed, that the senator is rooting for us. Who knew he was such a sap behind that asshole facade?"

"They usually are. Obviously, you need to read more of my books," I murmured, taking a glance at my inbox. Messages requesting interviews, offering services, and representation filled the screen. This would take days to sort through.

"I . . . I don't know what to say."

"This is a perfect example of how, with the right spin, some scenarios that seemed so dire in one light can look completely different in another."

My phone vibrated in my hand, and I looked down to see Laurel's name appear on the screen. I opened her message.

LAUREL

Since both you and Brandt decided to not show for work today, it fell to me to write a statement for the senator to put out around this bullshit romance author hullabaloo.

I think I might have a future in it. Maybe I'll apply for the vacancy when you quit to chase this author career of yours full time.

From the office of Senator Mitchell Marsden: *While this office does not comment on the personal lives of its staff members, it does comment when the patriarchy is being upheld to unreasonable standards. When someone chooses to write, in their free time, about the consensual owning by fictional characters of their sexuality, they take back the power of those who identify with those characters little by little. This office is appalled that a member of the press would engage in a smear campaign about the alleged activities of a staff member in their personal life, and* *suggests that outlet get a life and engage in some real reporting for a change.*

I laughed wetly, showing Preston the screen.

"She's not wrong. She does have the senator's voice down pat. Maybe I should stop trying to censor him so much," he mused.

"I know he said I'd have a place on his staff for as long as I wanted it, but I have to admit, I didn't believe it. I've been kicked out on my ass for far less."

"He's a man of his word. And also, he wasn't kidding about gunning for that romance reader vote. He'll take gaining any population he can get."

I laughed again before sighing.

"Well, I guess I have a decision to make," I said, tapping the back of my phone as I glanced around the room before my eyes landed on Preston's.

"Not that I am trying to influence your decision, but I think you should go public."

I waved my hand. "Oh yeah, that's definitely going to happen. I should probably hire a publicist with my new royalty spike to help, but that's not what I'm talking about."

"What decision then?"

My phone rang before I could answer him, with Michelle calling this time.

"Hi, Michelle."

"Hey, Jax. Just got finished with prepping everything for tomorrow. How are you holding up? Preston find his way there yet?"

"He's actually standing here right now," I said. Had everyone expected he would come chasing after me? I was the only one too scared to trust in what we had?

"Figured. Well, I'm on my way back now, just need to stop at the drugstore to grab something really quick. So you know, if you're going to have sex on my couch, make it a quickie."

"We are not going to have sex on your couch, Mich."

Preston's eyes widened and then looked at me with interest. I smacked him gently on the arm.

"Whatever you say. You're welcome to stay with me as long as you need, but make sure he knows that my moving your boxes was a onetime thing. He's got to get you out of there without my help."

I laughed, fully believing she would sit on the couch and watch us carrying things before lifting another finger.

"I'll be sure he knows. See you soon."

"Toodles."

He looked at me quizzically.

"Michelle says you're responsible for getting my boxes back out of here. She maxes out at one move."

"Does that mean . . ." He tried to keep his face neutral, but I detected the hopefulness in his voice.

"I think it's time for me to be brave and not so afraid of the future and what it might bring. I might not be great at it. I might still have moments of doubt and panic. But I'd like that future to be spent with you, for as long as you'll have me."

"That's great. But you robbed me of a chance to use my line." He actually crossed his arms and pouted. It was adorable.

"Go ahead." I interlocked my hands in front of me, waiting.

"Jax, will you marry me? Because I'd like to date you."

I burst out in laughter. "Did you just quote *The Proposal* at me?"

"I've fallen asleep to that movie at least once a week for the past two months, so yes. And besides, who wouldn't want to be Ryan Reynolds, even if just for a moment?"

"You're a nerd, Brandt."

"And you wouldn't have me any other way." He closed the gap between us, pulling me into his arms and bending down to put his lips on mine. After a moment, he pulled back, saying, "So, about that couch sex . . ."

I pushed him away. "Definitely not. There's no chance one of your brothers has a truck or something, right? I'm going to tank my profile rating using ride shares to cart my stuff all over the city."

"I bet Duncan has someone who can help us out. I'll give him a call."

Preston did that while I gathered the few things I had unpacked since yesterday's mad dash. I felt a little sheepish about the whole thing, but I think in some ways I needed Preston to come after me. That sounded dramatic and a bit self-centered, but after having to fight for myself for so long, having someone else fight to keep me might have been necessary.

"He's going to have someone here within the hour," Preston reported as I grabbed toiletries from the bathroom.

"Oh, that's great. Let him know I owe him one."

"He already knows. He says he has us signed up for volunteer events from now until forever."

I laughed. "I can think of worse things. At least we'll be together."

Preston's smile was as close to the definition of "from ear to ear" as I'd ever seen in real life.

"So let's go be together on the couch while we wait for Duncan's ride?" Preston waggled his eyebrows, somehow moving them independently of each other.

"Fine, but only hand stuff. No one wants someone else's naked ass on their couch," I said, trying to sound exasperated, but eager to get my hands on Preston too. Emotional declarations of affection were growing more comfortable for me, but that didn't mean I wanted to stop the physical ones anytime soon. Not having to wait until we got back home wasn't the worst idea in the world.

Home. That word again. As Preston pulled me down to his lap, feeling the safety in his arms around me, I knew I found my home in him.

Twenty~Five

JAX

NOVEMBER

The week my story broke, I made an agreement with the senator that I would go down to part time until the election. Now that the campaign was ending, Senator Marsden could promote from campaign employees to fill any vacancies left on his DC-based staff. Preston and I decided we wouldn't ask him about the Buzzfeed article, and he never offered any hints confirming he tipped off Katie. I did catch him reading *Wild and Wicked*, the first book in my most popular series, on a flight shortly afterward though, so I think it's safe to assume it was him.

I found a therapist as one of my first acts with my part-time schedule. My tendency to bolt when events created upheaval and the way it related back to the loss of my parents and grandma wasn't something I should grapple with alone, especially with Preston in my life. He even joined me for a few sessions so we could work on our communication and talk through how my leaving had affected him. I hated knowing it hurt him, and appreciated the opportunity to talk through it with a professional.

Preston and I started referring to each other as partners, instead of fiancés. Even though I moved back in with him, I didn't put the ring back on. We decided we wanted me to wear the ring because it was right for us, not because we had made an agreement over wine and French food when we barely knew each other. So not quite a Sandy and Ryan level move to keep dating each other, but our own spin on it. We eventually told all his brothers the truth. Hayden took it the hardest. Duncan threatened to make us plan the next service event for BII in "all our spare time." But when they saw nothing in our relationship changed except a ring, they accepted things and moved on.

Election night arrived on a crisp night in Rhode Island. The energy at our election night party buzzed cautiously optimistic. As the senator predicted, we took a slight hit in the polls after *The Dispatch's* story ran. We recovered from it stronger than before after Senator Marsden demolished his opponent in their debate last summer. It honestly wasn't even fair, and I almost felt for his opponent when I caught him crying in the wings after the event. But then I remembered he called me a hussy for what I wrote, and I got over that in no time.

None of the rest of Preston's family could make the trip tonight, but that didn't mean they weren't making their support known. A group chat had officially been set up for the brothers and their partners. Charlotte and I looked forward to some more non-Brandt energy joining the thread. We were hopeful another addition was right around the corner.

DUNCAN

My assistant is keeping me up to date and says the exit poll numbers look strong.

HUNTER

Seriously, you can't track that yourself?

DUNCAN

What else are assistants for?

HAYDEN

My boss, ladies and gents.

But getting back on track, Char and I have ordered take out and are glued to MSNBC. We keep looking for you guys in the crowd.

CHARLOTTE

I keep looking. Hayden keeps eating.

SPENCER

Make sure you give the senator a good luck kiss for me. He looks handsome in his suit.

PRESTON

Making note to self to get him a restraining order against you before you move to DC.

JAX

I dunno. I think he's got a shot.

SPENCER

Meh, maybe. Maybe not. I think I've had enough of the over-controlling type in my life for a while. DC is my oyster. Let the bi boy run free.

JAX

We'll definitely need to be sure we're in town for Pride next June.

★　★　★

Preston and I were moving to Massachusetts in January so he could get involved in the local community and launch his campaign in his home state later next year. We found a cute little place in the Sixth Congressional District that had a home office for each of us and allowed pets. Preston adorably thought we were getting a dog, but I knew at heart we're both cat people. Spencer planned to move into Preston's studio. We hoped to be able to hang onto it until the election in two years.

"Preston, *The Providence Times* wants you for a quote about the senator's speech at the fall festival last week." Laurel walked over, a headset in one ear and a clipboard in hand.

"Duty calls," he said, giving me a kiss on the cheek and walking over to the reporter in question, shaking their hand and putting on his politician's smile. I loved all of his smiles, but that one in particular could make me do anything he wanted. I banned him from using it all but once a week whenever I realized I had done the laundry four weeks in a row.

"So, you ready to sign up for another six years of this?" I gestured at the party with my glass of wine. Laurel looked around thoughtfully.

"I think I am, or at least the start of it. Caitlin's talking about marriage and kids, but is getting promoted next year. We each want to attempt to carry a child, so I think I'll go first, knock on wood." She knocked on the back of her clipboard. "So who knows if I'll make it the full six years, but I also no longer want to ring the senator's neck on a daily basis, so maybe I will."

"Weekly though still, right?" I said conspiratorially.

"Absolutely." She grinned back. "How are you feeling about the move? Ready for what comes next?"

"I am." I looked back and forth, making sure no one nearby was paying us any attention. "My agent sold my next book series to a traditional publisher, under my real name. It's a small-town sapphic cowgirl romance."

"Jax! That's amazing. I'm so proud of you, and also want you to send it to me ASAP. But does this mean the paranormal series you were telling me about is dead? Because I so want to read about the alien senator falling in love with a human girl."

I laughed. "Not dead. We put in the contract I could

continue publishing paranormal independently. So don't worry, you'll get your alien romance."

"And if your alien senator happens to look like a senator we love to hate, I won't be the one to tell him."

I sipped my drink conspiratorially. There was no telling where inspiration would strike.

Preston rejoined us, slipping his arm around my waist, pulling me back against his chest.

"What are we talking about, ladies?"

"Aliens, romance, senators. The usual," I answered, gazing up at his handsome face.

"Ah, your books then." Preston smiled knowingly. Having someone to brainstorm with in person was new, but we were having a lot of fun, too.

Laurel covered the ear not wearing an electronic contraption and tapped the earpiece, listening closely.

"Gotta go. Alien senator, I mean Senator Marsden, wants his dinner before the polls close. And then he wants to see you, Preston, to go over the speeches one last time." She took off like a shot, dodging people effortlessly, brushing no one in the crowded room.

"Speeches? I thought you only wrote the victory speech?" I looked up at Preston.

"I did." He looked back at me with that eyebrow waggle I loved so much. "He just doesn't know it yet."

I laughed, clasping Preston's hand around my waist with my free one. "He's going to be so mad."

"Nah, I'll just tell him I knew he wasn't going to lose. It'll pump up his ego. Besides, what's he going to do, fire me?"

I turned and looked him in the eyes, my tone more serious. "How are you? Last speech before it's your turn. You've avoided the question every time I've asked for the last week."

He smiled softly at me. "Earlier this week, I didn't have an answer for you. Tonight? I'm okay. I'm ready for whatever comes next."

I stepped into Preston's arms, stretching up on my tiptoes for a light peck before pulling back to meet his eyes.

"That makes two of us."

Epilogue

PRESTON

TWO YEARS LATER

What a week. We knew when Jax's publisher picked the first of November as her book's pub date in an election year, we would be running ourselves ragged. Now that the week had arrived, we were operating mostly on adrenaline and caffeine. I rushed across Salem from a campaign event ahead of the school board meeting to Toil and Trouble Books, who was playing host to Jax's launch event.

I looked at my watch and swore, glancing up at the immobile traffic to clear. Halloween was over. Why were there still so many people in town?

"You can just let me out here," I said to the rideshare driver.

"Whatever you need, sir," he responded, turning his four-way flashers on.

"Thanks," I said, sliding out of the car and squeezing between two parked cars to hit the sidewalk. Walking briskly the final few blocks, I stopped outside the store to wipe the sweat gathered there despite the cool New England fall air. After cleaning off the glasses I tried to protest I hadn't needed, but did make life so much easier, I took a peek inside the window. A huge smile broke out on my face. The store was packed. And Jax thought no one would show up.

I opened the door and showed my ticket to the employee scanning them just inside. Jax tried to insist I didn't need a ticket. She would put me on a list. Why she thought I wouldn't take every opportunity to support her opening week numbers was beyond me. That's my girl, that's my lady, and I'm proud of that.

Charlotte waved to me from the front row and indicated the empty seat next to her. I weaved through the crowd to embrace my sister-in-law to be.

"Can you believe this crowd?" she squealed, her face expressing pure glee at the book loving community gathered around. "And she thought no one would come."

"That's what I said," I said, laughing. "How's she doing? Nervous? Did she get my tea delivery?"

Charlotte nodded. "She did. I caught her swooning a little bit when she realized you ordered it ahead. But I'm sure she'd deny it if I called her on it."

A woman stepped to the front of the store, where all our chairs were oriented and a hush fell over the crowd as it tends to in a group of well-trained adults.

"Welcome to Toil and Trouble and thank you for joining us to celebrate the launch of *Ride 'em, Cowgirl* by Jax Carter." She led everyone in a round of applause, a few whoops breaking out among the crowd. "My name is Joanie and I'm the Events Manager here at T&T. Just a smidge of housekeeping. While we know things always stay a little *witchy* here in Salem, now that Halloween is officially over, it's not too early to start thinking about your holiday shopping. Every purchase for the month of November comes with a coupon for free ice skating at the Holly Ridge Holiday Festival, located only a couple hours away from here."

Charlotte shot me a wink; her best friend planned the holiday festival in the town where my dad and Margaret now lived. She had Charlotte offer all the indie bookstores in the tri-state area these coupons. Jax and I were going to take advantage of our newfound proximity to check it out—Jax had coordinated with Ridge Reads to do a signing next month.

After reading Jax's bio, Joanie said, "And without further ado, please welcome Jax Carter!"

The applause and cheers were plentiful as Jax walked around the corner where she had been waiting, waving at the crowd. As she stepped up to the podium, her eyes snagged mine. I mouthed, "I love you," my chest warming as her smile got even larger before she broke my gaze, turning her attention to the rest of the crowd.

"Wow, there sure are a lot of you here. My fiancé and future sister-in-law will tell you I thought no one was going to show up." The crowd laughed appropriately.

"But seriously, it means a lot to me that you're here. As little as two years ago, I wasn't sure I would ever be able to stand up in front of a crowd and claim my work. While I'm not sure I would recommend to anyone the way my work was exposed," she paused while a few mutters emitted from those who had followed Jax/June's career prior to this release. "I won't regret what it's done for me in terms of standing up loud and proud, and saying I write romance, and anyone who has a problem with it can go—" Jax paused again.

"Am I allowed to swear up here? It's my first time," she asked. Joanie laughed, nodding. Jax continued. "Well, they can go fuck themselves."

The loudest cheer yet erupted, and I may have contributed a wolf whistle to the cause. Once everyone had simmered down, Jax held up the book, an illustration of two cowgirls in an embrace in front of a scenic background on the cover. The ring of the fourth finger of her left hand caught the light, but the diamond's reflection dimmed compared to the look of joy on Jax's face.

"Let's hear a little bit from these two cowgirls, shall we? I promise, no spoilers. Chapter one, Layla: They say never look a gift horse in the mouth, but what if that horse walks right up to you and neighs in your face?"

From there she was off, the crowd laughing at her witty one-liners and groaning in disappointment when she stopped for the question and answer portion of the evening. She first answered questions Joanie had prepared, before opening things up to the audience. Jax answered questions about the difference between indie and traditional publishing, whether she would continue to write under June Kennedy, and what she had planned next.

"I think we have time for one more question," Joanie said as she and Jax exchanged what could only be described as a conspiratorial glance. Charlotte's hand raised beside me, increasing my suspicion they were up to something.

"Yes, you there in the front." Jax pointed to Charlotte.

"As someone who obviously cares a lot about the local community and supporting local businesses, by choosing to have your launch party at an independent bookstore, do you have any comments about the upcoming Election Day?"

My cheeks warmed and I willed myself to not turn red.

"I do, in fact. If you're visiting from outside of Salem, you may not know that my fiancé, Preston Brandt, is running for our local state Senate seat in next week's election. Preston, would you come up here?"

Charlotte led a round of applause that was far more lackluster than any Jax had garnered so far that night.

"Do you have anything you want to say to your future constituents and honored guests?" Jax handed me the microphone, and I took it begrudgingly.

"Hi, I am Preston Brandt, and I am running for the district's state Senate seat. I'd appreciate your support if you're voting next week, but this is Jax's night and I don't want to take away from it . . ." I glanced back in her direction and read the command in her gaze only a former Communications Director could give to someone screwing up an opportunity for free face-time with their voters.

"But, after you've supported this lovely bookstore and gotten any books signed and pictures taken, if you wanted to stop by and chat, I'll be over there." I pointed at a corner that seemed out of the way enough it wouldn't clog up the flow of traffic, though I was sure no one would take me up on the offer.

"Jax and I moved here almost two years ago because I planned to run for the House of Representatives. While representing the state of Massachusetts in Congress is still a goal of mine, once I got here and began to really know this area and the people in it, I knew I wanted the chance to live in the community I was elected by on a more regular basis first. So again, buy books, so Jax can sign them, and then, if you're not exhausted and ready to head home, you can see me."

Jax lead a more enthusiastic round of applause as I walked over to my area. Joanie gave instructions on forming the signing line, and the crowd started to fold up chairs and disperse, some to the cash register, some to browse, and some got right in line to be among the first to chat with the woman of the hour.

Charlotte made her way to me. "Sorry, she asked me to do it."

I looked at her and shook my head. "You don't look very sorry."

"I guess I'm not." She shrugged. "I want you to win, and I agreed with Jax that you had an opportunity here. This time next year, I'll officially be a Brandt, you know. I have to support my team."

"So that means you all decided where to do the wedding?" I asked. Hayden and Charlotte were having a tough time deciding whether they wanted to get married in Holly Ridge or in Washington, DC.

She laughed and shook her head. "Not even a little bit. But we did decide we wanted a wedding in September, so we'll have to make a decision soon. I know Blaire would take care of a lot of the planning if we did it in Holly Ridge, but Duncan has offered to hire a wedding planner if we do it in DC."

I snorted. "Of course he has."

"My Mom and I have a plan to sit down and talk things out over Thanksgiving this year. Maybe I'll make her decide." Charlotte tapped her chin, musing over that idea when her eyes caught on something behind me. "But I'm going to go circulate. I am technically here for work. I think you have a few people wanting to take you up on that offer." She flashed me one more smile before moving into the crowd and striking up a conversation with another book lover.

I turned around and tried my best to hide my shock at the small group that waited for me. "Hi," I said, sticking my hand out to the man closest to my left. "Preston Brandt, nice to meet you."

"I'm Billy. My daughter Olivia loves Jax's books, so we drove in to catch the event. I think sixteen is a bit too young for adult romance books, but she picked up her mom's collection after her mom passed a few years ago." He shrugged. "I can't break that connection—it's one of the parts of her mom she's got left, you know?"

I nodded. "I do know. Olivia and Jax will have a lot to chat about. She got her start with her grandma's collection."

Billy shot a look at the line, his face brightening with a smile when he found who he was looking for. "She's there in the purple shirt, with that whole stack of books to be signed. So while she's waiting, I thought I'd asked you a few more questions about your plans for assisting first-generation college students."

And with that, we were off. As the store emptied, several more people stopped by to say hello, ask a question, or even wish me luck in the election next week. Charlotte waved from the door, the look on her face saying she didn't want to interrupt, as she headed out to drive to the next town on her Massachusetts independent bookstore tour.

Eventually the store emptied of everyone but Jax and me and a few employees. They waved us out after Jax finished signing the rest of their stock of her books.

"Have I told you how proud of you I am?" I asked as we left the store, almost ninety minutes after Jax started signing books. We turned to the left, walking toward our car.

"I think only approximately fifty-three times, but I could hear it once more," she teased, her eyes sparkling in the reflection of the streetlights lining the sidewalk.

"I'm so proud. These people came to see you, they waited in line, wanted to tell you how much your books have meant to them. You're making a difference in people's lives, telling stories where people can see themselves reflected. Your grandma would be so proud."

Jax blinked through her tears. She dedicated this book to her grandma, something that had resonated with a lot of readers online who grew up stealing their grandma's romance novels off the shelves too.

While Jax was no longer as averse to emotional moments and we talked a lot about our memories of our loved ones we lost, I knew this was a night for celebrating. I tried to pick the mood back up.

"Let's go home and you can ride me, cowgirl?"

She groaned, wiping her eyes, a grateful smiling crossing her face. "Okay, that's it. That joke will officially expire at midnight tonight. Release day is over. That was the deal."

I laughed, throwing my arm around her shoulder, bringing her to my side and laying a kiss on the crown of her head. "Okay, fine. You're right, I promised."

She wrapped her arm around my lower back. "And just remember, after next week, you'll be Mr. State Senator, and I'll be the concerned constituent you need to assuage." Jax gave her voice a fake breathy quality, twirling her free hand in her hair.

I laughed. "Did you use an anagram for sausage on purpose? If so, well done."

Jax took a little bow.

"And c'mon, don't jinx me. There's a lot of race left to go," I continued.

Jax stepped in front of me, her hands on my face.

"You're right. You haven't won yet, but I believe in you, and I know everyone sees what I see. A caring man who is dedicated to his principles and will give his all to represent the people who elected him. That's what they want, not someone who's doing to take away their rights and smoke cigars down at the good old boys club."

I let out a breath. "I sure hope so."

Jax pulled me down for a kiss. After a moment, I broke away. We stood there for a moment, our gazes locked. I counted myself lucky I got stood up in the Capitol Visitors Center that day. The story of how we got here may not be like anyone else's, but it was perfectly and uniquely ours.

We started walking again, Jax's arm looped through mine this time.

"So, what else do you see in me?" I asked, my voice light and teasing.

"The type of stallion this cowgirl can't wait to mount," she said, drawling in a terrible country accent. We laughed the last few feet to the car. I opened the passenger door for Jax to climb in and navigated to the driver's side. Starting the car, Jax connected her phone to the audio system.

"I know we haven't set a date or anything, but I did have a suggestion for our first dance."

"Yeah, what's that?" I asked, looking over at her expectantly.

She swiped across her screen a few times, and the opening chords played to a song that never failed to put a smile on my face. Not being able to resist though, I played dumb.

"Why, what's this song?" I asked, putting the car in gear and pulling out onto the road.

"This is the first song we ever danced to, in your apartment the day I moved in. Oh, if those kids could see us now." I caught her look over at me in my peripheral vision. "You really didn't rem—" She paused as she caught the size of my shit-eating grin. She shoved my leg gently. "You remember."

"Of course I remember. How could I forget the first time I got to dance with the most beautiful girl in the world?"

She laughed, putting her hand back on my leg, but leaving it to rest there this time.

"Take me home, Mr. Brandt."

"As you wish."

Acknowledgments

This book was a labor of love, with so many people to thank.

Thank you to my lived experience beta readers: Ashley, Julie, Lori, Samantha, and Shannon. Your feedback made this book so much better and I'm so grateful for your time and care.

Allie, Darrah, Izzy, Kelly, and Steph - thank you for being some of my earliest readers, for your spot-on feedback, and for all your love and support along the way.

Lacey and Cassie - thanks for being cheerleaders *and* making sure I know where commas go and how many brothers Preston has.

Rachel, I'm so thankful that book journal put our January releases next to each other and that we're navigating this author life together.

To all my friends and loved ones who learn new terms and root for me always, you keep me going. To my Bookstagram friends who have become the first to sign-up for cover reveals and ARCs, I couldn't do it without you.

Chloe Liese was the first author to show me tummy troubles had a place in a romance novel, along with every other facet of a person's being, and I'm forever grateful.

And to you, dear reader, whether this is your first book of mine, you were in my DMs with your guesses for who the next Brandt Brother would be after Capitally Matched, or you've been here since Carry Me Through Christmas, I'm so thankful for you. You let me carry out this dream.

Rachel grew up in Western PA and found her love of reading early in life, supported by her parents with frequent trips to the library and local bookstores. She stumbled into the online bookish world in late 2020 diving headfirst into the Romance genre. In 2021, she changed careers and took a job at a bookstore and started her first official novel-length writing project.

Now Rachel is getting an MFA in Popular Fiction at Seton Hill University and juggling too many story ideas for one brain to handle. She's excited to continue to share Happily Ever Afters with you that bring the laughs and the love.

When not immersed in her bookish world, you can find Rachel hanging out with her husband and two cats, spending time with friends in the Washington DC area, and rooting for Pittsburgh sports teams.

HOLLY RIDGE SERIES

Carry Me Through Christmas

Coming Soon: Make You Mine This Christmas

THE BRANDT BROTHERS SERIES

Capitally Matched

Capitally Engaged

Capitally Unexpected

Coming Soon: Capitally Yours